A SCENT OF LILAC

Also By Elizabeth Law:

Double Deception

A SCENT
OF LILAC

Elizabeth Law

Walker and Company
New York

Library of Congress Cataloging-in-Publication Data

Law, Elizabeth.
  A scent of lilac / Elizabeth Law.
    p.   cm.
  ISBN 0-8027-1010-7
  I. Title.
PS3562.A857S3   1988   87-27699   813'.54—dc19

First published in the United States of America in 1988 by Walker Publishing Company,
Inc.

Published simultaneously in Canada by Thomas Allen & Son
Canada, Limited, Markham, Ontario.

Printed in the United States of America

10 9 8 7 6 5 4 3 2 1

A SCENT OF LILAC

=1=

LILAC MARY MORTON was growing into a beauty. Nobody
had gone so far as to tell her so since, in the Lameter
household, vanity and worldliness were gently but firmly
discouraged. Still, she had only to look in her mirror to see
the evidence.

It was true she was of middling height and lacked the
plumpness that was fashionable, but the whiteness of her
skin, the eyes that were almost the same shade as her name,
the wealth of blue-black hair which hung like a shining
cloak to her waist had an exotic quality that raised her
above conventional prettiness. There had been a period
when she sighed for a Cupid's bow mouth and blond curls
such as adorned the head of her best friend, Amelia Watson; but, now that Lilac had reached the age of seventeen,
she had the sense to notice that, though people might rave
about Amelia's prettiness, their eyes lingered on her.

There was no celebration to mark Lilac's birthday. As
far back as she could remember, there had never been. One
did not, her Grandmother Lameter explained, celebrate
the death of one's mama. Mama had died in childbirth just
after Lilac came into the world.

"Living only long enough to name you for her favorite
flower," Grandmother had told her. "Her heart was broken
when those savages killed your poor papa."

Grandmother's eyes always filled with tears when she
spoke of that terrible time, as Lilac's own eyes brimmed in
sympathy. She didn't actually feel any real emotion, since

1

it is difficult to mourn a portrait framed in black with a posy of flowers always before it. The face that looked out of the frame was delicate and heart-shaped. Fair ringlets bunched at each side from a centre parting, and the eyes exactly like Lilac's.

She had no portrait of Papa, but Grandmother had described him. "Tall and dark, my love, with regular features. He was quiet in his manner, but he burned with zeal for the Lord and died a martyr."

"It was all very noble and sad but it was also a lot to live up to. Whenever Lilac got into mischief, which she frequently did as a child, Grandmother would reproach her with a reminder that Mama and Papa were watching and weeping from Heaven.

"I thought there wasn't any weeping in heaven," Lilac demurred in response.

That had been on the occasion when she took advantage of a ladder left outside the house by a careless workman and shinned up to the roof to find out if St Paul's Cathedral was visible from that height. It was not only the danger of the escapade which had horrified her grandmother but also the fact that, in order to attain her goal, Lilac had removed her skirt and climbed in her drawers. That was something little ladies of twelve simply didn't do.

There had been other incidents as well, though none so shocking. Meanwhile, Lilac gained the definite impression that by now Heaven was awash with the tears of poor Papa and Mama.

"You must never forget that your mama was a saint," Grandmother said. "Even when she was small her piety was quite remarkable."

Lilac's piety, on the other hand, wasn't at all remarkable. Of course, she attended prayers every morning and knelt, listening to Grandmother read the lesson, with Cook and Alice and Mr. Briggs on chairs in the rear. On Sundays Lilac went to church where she sat with Grandmother in the Lameter pew, which had been designed for the large family Philip Lameter had hoped to found a hundred years before.

"Unhappily only one child survived out of a family of six," Grandmother told her. "That child, Silas, had two sons."

The elder of those two had been Jeremy, who settled down as a man of business and married Grandmother. She was not a grandmother then, of course, but Miss Barbara Lovell—eighteen years old and delicately pretty in her hooped skirt, with a modest income inherited from her parents—altogether a suitable bride for a sober, ambitious man past thirty.

But there had been only one child of that union, the saintly Mary; and Jeremy Lameter had died when his daughter was only fourteen.

"Which was rather unfortunate," Grandmother confided. "There was an entail or some such thing on the property which your grandpapa had neglected to consider, and everything went to dear Jeremy's younger brother, Philip."

She pursed her lips whenever she mentioned Philip, who had always been something of a rakehell, and never married or settled down but, instead, went off to shoot tigers in India and climb pyramids in Egypt. He had put the business in the hands of a capable manager, given his widowed sister-in-law leave to stay on in the family home, and departed to lead his ramshackle, unsatisfactory life, thereafter descending upon London only at irregular intervals. Lilac had seen him but two or three times in her life and was, on those occasions, very much in awe of the tall gentleman who wore an old-fashioned periwig and helped himself to snuff from a box having on its ivory lid a carving of a lady with no clothes on at all. He was not, apparently, very fond of children and surveyed her through his quizzing glass for a long time before promising darkly, "There'll be trouble with this one before very long."

"Environment has a tremendous influence," Grandmother had said in a sharp tone.

"Let us hope." He reached into his pocket for a gold sovereign, which he put into Lilac's hand, then waved away her thanks with an air that suggested he was already bored with her.

Environment was what one grew up in, and heredity was what one received from one's parents. Considering that, Lilac decided that she certainly hadn't inherited her mother's saintliness, though she did have her eyes. Lilac's features were stronger and more definite than Mary's had been, her cheekbones higher, her mouth wider, and Grandmother said she was an inch or so taller. Of course, it was possible Lilac took after her father's family, though she knew little about them save that they came from Yorkshire.

Meanwhile, life went along pleasantly enough in the tall, narrow house Great-great-grandfather Philip Lameter had built when he returned from Cathay with a consignment of silks and jade and hopes of founding a dynasty. The house itself had been elegant once, with high, moulded ceilings and beautifully carved furniture; but Grandmother's taste ran to velvet drapes, dozens of ornaments, and samplers with religious mottoes on them.

There were times when Lilac felt pressed in and stifled: a feeling which had grown steadily in her ever since she left the exclusive day school where she, Amelia, and a score of young ladies had been given sufficient education to ensure they were not illiterate, but not so much that it would frighten away any prospective husbands. Lilac had been a good student. She enjoyed reading and writing essays. She had acquitted herself well in the weekly dancing class; but she had no gift for playing any instrument, took no pleasure in making watercolour sketches of vases of flowers, and tangled up the silks when she was constrained to do a little needlework.

"The truth is," she told Amelia who had come to tea, "I

haven't any accomplishments at all. It's fortunate I won't have to earn my living as a governess, for I would never find a situation."

"You will be married for your looks," Amelia said without envy. "One glance from those eyes, and the gentlemen will fight duels."

"I only know Mr Fellowes, the curate; and I cannot picture him fighting a duel about anything," Lilac said, her lips twitching. "Except, perhaps, with a stick of celery; and, even then, he'd surrender after the first blow."

"Poor Mr Fellowes." Amelia made languishing eyes. "But there will be some gentlemen at the supper party next week. Alfred has sworn to me that he will bring some of his friends."

Amelia's brother was a lieutenant in the East India regiment and visited his family when his gambling debts became insupportable.

"Your grandmother has given you leave to come, hasn't she?" Amelia said now. "I know we are not out yet, but this is a very informal affair."

"I sometimes wonder if I want to come out at all," Lilac said.

"Not come out?" Amelia gaped at her friend in horror. "But you can't possibly stay in the schoolroom forever. You will wither away into a spinster."

"Oh, I don't believe I would enjoy that," Lilac said promptly. "It is only that . . . Don't you ever wish you didn't know what was going to happen next month and the month after that?"

"But I don't know that," Amelia said bewildered.

"I'm not talking about the details," Lilac said impatiently. "I mean that we *do* know the general course our lives will take, and there isn't any way to alter it. It's as if we had boarded the stage and, though we are not conversant with all the scenery, we know the names of the towns we'll pass through and the final destination."

"That makes me feel very secure," Amelia said placidly.

"I will meet somebody suitable and marry him, and we will live in a charming house and have children."

"I suppose so. I only feel there ought to be something more." Lilac demurred.

"One might marry an officer and go with him to some far-flung outpost," Amelia said. "But very unpleasant things happen in those places sometimes. One might be mur—." She broke off, flushing slightly as she remembered that her friend's father had been murdered by savages. Lilac, however, said cheerfully, "One might be murdered in London, too, if one ventured into the wrong part of the city. What are you going to wear?"

"Blue, I expect. My new dress with the lace inserts." Amelia sounded complacent.

"Then I shall wear my new, pink dress."

That dress hung under wraps in the capacious wardrobe and was the first really grown-up dress Lilac had ever owned. Grandmother had been doubtful.

"I cannot imagine when you will find occasion to wear such a frivolous garment," she said. But then she had yielded, moved by the pleading in her granddaughter's eyes. Perhaps a little frivolity could do no harm occasionally; and Lilac did look exquisite in the narrow, ruffled skirt that flowed from a tiny bodice with frilled sleeves and a low neckline dipped daringly below the collarbone.

"Perhaps Alfred will fall in love with you," Amelia suggested. "Then, when you are wed, you can follow him to Calcutta."

Lilac smiled vaguely by way of reply. She would rather enjoy travelling to a foreign country, but not if it meant having to marry Amelia's brother. Alfred cultivated a dashing moustache and didn't seem to have enough energy left from that for any other activity. Indeed, she suspected the glory of the pink dress would be wasted on him, but that didn't prevent her from looking forward to wearing it.

"Frederick will have to take you," her grandmother said when Amelia had left and the final arrangements were being made. "I expect you to be home by midnight, so he will return and pick you up at a quarter to the hour."

"They probably won't serve supper until eleven," Lilac protested.

"Then you will have plenty of time in which to partake of it before Frederick collects you."

Barbara Lameter's voice was firm. When she spoke thus it was useless to argue. She was a small woman who had recently put on more weight than her doctor liked, but food was the only area of her life in which she was undisciplined. Behind the gold-rimmed spectacles perched on her nose her grey eyes were resolute.

"It seems so foolish," Lilac said. "To get out the carriage for the purpose of travelling six streets."

"You are not proposing to walk there, I hope?"

"I suppose not." Lilac heaved an involuntary sigh.

Ladies seldom walked anywhere during the day, and after dark they never went on foot. Even in the middle-class areas, where the houses had high railings and long gardens at the back, the streets were considered to be teeming with unknown perils.

"I think it a trifle odd of the Watsons to give a party when there is no special occasion to warrant it," her grandmother was saying.

"They would have invited you, but they know you never go anywhere," Lilac said.

"Fortunately I have sufficient resources in myself not to be forever gadding about in search of entertainment," the other said tartly.

"Alfred may be drafted out to India at any moment."

"A promise he has been making ever since he got his commission but has not yet honoured. Oh, very well. I will cease my strictures on my neighbours, and you will cease drumming up reasons why you should remain after mid-night."

"Thank you, Grandmother."

Lilac didn't kiss her since the affection between them

was seldom demonstrated. Still, she glowed with pleasure, and her quick step was light as she went out of the room.

Barbara Lameter, looking after her, bit her lip and allowed a brief frown to pucker her brow. The girl was growing up too quickly, becoming difficult to protect; and Barbara was determined to protect her as she had failed in the end to protect Mary.

Mary had been Barbara's finest creation. Her disappointment at being told there would be no more children after the birth of her daughter was tempered by the resolve that she could now spend all her energies in the protection of this one, beloved child. Mary had been a biddable little girl, always ready to sacrifice her pocket money for the sake of the heathen, looking like an apprentice angel as she knelt to say her prayers with the lamplight outlining her golden head. When Jeremy reproached Barbara for their lack of sons, she could always remind him that they had a daughter whose sweetness and goodness were the cause of much admiring comment among the neighbours.

Then Jeremy had most inconsiderately died without making any provision for her or for Mary. The house, the business, and most of the income had reverted to Philip, who did not appreciate them in the least. It was, perhaps, ungrateful of her to think like that since he had been so generous, giving her a life tenancy in the house and a handsome allowance. He'd even spoken of launching his niece into Society. That prospect alarmed Barbara considerably, for she dreaded that Mary might be contaminated by the world.

Fortunately, Philip had been absent on one of his protracted trips when Robert Morton came into the district and Mary met him at a church bazaar. A minister of Northern stock with a burning desire to convert the heathen Indian tribes, his face shone as he talked of his vocation. Mary had sat as close as propriety allowed, drinking in his words.

"I need a wife," he'd said. "I have needed a wife for a

long time, but I would not marry where I could not love. The two of us together in the savage wilderness without love to bind us would never succeed."

Mary had fallen in love with him more rapidly than her mother dared hope; and the wedding followed almost immediately, a quiet affair with the bride tremulously lovely in white satin.

Robert Morton took his bride up to Yorkshire to meet his family, after which they were to sail to the Americas. Barbara's most precious possession would be borne thousands of miles away into unknown dangers. It was a life that would have suited Barbara herself; and, though it was painful to let go, she had felt as if she were realising her own ambitions through her child.

Then, like a thunderbolt came the terrible news. Following that, Mary had returned, a pale, small ghost with blue eyes staring out of a white face. She had not wanted to talk. Only the prospect of the coming child had pleased her, though in the end she had lived only long enough to whisper that it was to be named Lilac.

Barbara had added Mary to her life, then proceeded to create an environment where this child too could develop as the mother had done; but, though Barbara strained every nerve, there was no denying that Lilac lacked meekness and at times her behaviour displayed an alarming propensity towards wildness. Her grandmother tried to close her eyes to the fact; but, still, there could be no question that Lilac was self-willed and stubborn. Sometimes Barbara shivered when she thought of what the future might hold.

=== 2 ===

THOUGH THE WATSONS lived only six streets away, their house was much bigger and grander than the Lameter house and stood back from the road behind a high wall.

Lilac, sitting bolt upright in the carriage, felt a shiver of excitement. It made no matter this was only a supper party and that, as she was not yet out, it wasn't even considered necessary to have a chaperone. Tonight was an informal occasion, and she had been invited because she was Amelia's friend. What did matter was that Lilac looked very lovely. Ruffles of pink silk frothed out below her high waistline. Her long hair was held back by a matching ribbon, and a simple gold locket lay in the hollow of her throat.

"I'll be back at a quarter to twelve, Miss," Frederick said, having received his orders from Grandmother.

Frederick doubled as footman since the Lameter ladies seldom rode out except to church or to do a little shopping. Time would have hung heavily on his hands if he hadn't had indoor duties as well. He didn't have much to do as footman either since Grandmother rarely entertained.

By contrast, the Watsons entertained frequently, being a large family with daughters to marry off and sons coming of age or going off with their regiments. This was the first time Lilac had been invited to an evening affair. The house looked different from its daytime self with all the chandeliers sparkling and Amelia, in her blue dress, pattering down the stairs to meet her friend.

"You can leave your cloak in my bedroom. Oh, do come quickly. There is something I must tell you or I will absolutely burst," she said in an excited whisper.

Lilac followed her up the stairs and along the passage. Amelia formerly shared a room with her sister, but Frances had married the previous year. Now Amelia had it to herself. She and Lilac often exchanged confidences there.

"Oh, your dress is sweet. Alfred will likely fall madly in love with you the moment he sees you," Amelia said in a great rush the instant the door was closed. "Do you think this dress is too childish? Yours is lower in the neck."

"Yours is lovely. What did you want to tell me?"

"Only that Alfred has brought home the most handsome young man you ever saw. He's in Alfred's regiment and he's . . . " Amelia rolled her eyes languishingly.

"He will be going to India then in a few weeks," said Lilac.

"Or months. They have not yet received definite embarkation orders. Many officers are encouraged to marry before they go to keep them steadier, Alfred says, though he has so far resisted the advice himself. But Peter, Lieutenant Peter Wentworth is his name, is anxious to be married. He intimated as much over tea, and Alfred gave me a most meaning look."

"But you are not yet out," Lilac reminded her.

"There is no absolute law which forbids marriage until one is out," Amelia said. "I think all the fuss and bother of being presented is not worth a fig."

"Last week you said it must be the most exciting thing in the world."

"Last week I had not met Lieutenant Peter Wentworth," Amelia said. "He has the most divine moustache, Lilac."

"You have fallen in love with a moustache. What will you do if he ever shaves it off?"

"Oh, don't tease! Tell me if you think he admires me. You are placed next to him at supper so you will be able to engage him in casual conversation. I am certain he has no fianceé else he would not have spoken so openly about hoping to be married before he sails to India."

"I will be very subtle," Lilac promised.

"It would be wonderful to have a June wedding." Amelia eyes were dreamy. "June is such a perfect month for weddings. Are you sure this dress isn't too childish?"

"Well, it doesn't make you look elderly," Lilac said, laughing. "You know perfectly well that you look charming. Shall we go down? While we are up here talking, the lieutenant may be falling in love with somebody else."

Amelia hastened to open the door after a last fleeting glance in her mirror. She was truly very pretty, Lilac thought; and, though she was not envious, she did feel a tremor of uneasiness. Her own appearance, which had previously pleased her so much, now struck her as too unusual. Her hair never had the vestige of a wave or curl, and her face lacked the plumpness of her friend's. Lilac bit back a sigh and followed along the passage and down the stairs.

The drawing room and music room were separated by double doors, but these had been folded back and the carpets rolled away to improvise a long room where six or seven couples could stand up together. Card tables had been set up in the parlour and, in the dining room, cutlery and wine goblets sparkled down both sides of a snowly cloth.

"There you are, Alfred." Amelia darted across to where her brother stood in conversation with a tall, blond officer. "You remember Lilac, don't you?"

"Your friend from school," he nodded.

"Heavens, that was ages ago," Amelia tinkled. "Lilac, this is our guest, Lieutenant Peter Wentworth. My friend, Miss Lilac Morton."

He was certainly handsome. Lilac, who had suspected her friend of exaggeration, looked up into eyes almost as darkly blue as her own and felt her hand taken in a warm clasp that lasted a second longer than etiquette would have approved.

"Miss Morton, it's a great pleasure to make your acquaintance."

He had a pleasant voice, warm like his hand, and below the luxuriant moustache his teeth gleamed white and even.

"Lieutenant." To her annoyance, she felt colour flaming in her cheeks as she withdrew her hand.

"Lilac is my dearest friend. We have no secrets from each other," Amelia said.

"Then I must take care never to say anything to one I don't wish the other to hear," he said.

"Sisters never have much to say that is worth the hearing anyway," Alfred said in a bored tone.

"I have no sisters, only two younger brothers," Peter Wentworth said.

"Then you have missed nothing," Alfred assured him.

"I would contradict you. Looking at these two young ladies I begin to think I have missed a great deal."

He was certainly practised at gallantry, Lilac thought. She heard Amelia let out a breathless little giggle and knew instinctively that was not the way to interest him. Her own blush was fading as she said lightly, "You must not attempt to turn our heads with compliments, Lieutenant, or you may have two broken hearts to mourn your going to India."

"They are beginning the polka," Amelia said, her small foot tapping. "Alfred, you simply must dance with Lilac. She is quite splendid at the polka."

"Delighted," said Alfred, crooking his arm.

Accepting, Lilac walked with him to the far end of the room where a three-part orchestra was tuning up. It was not strictly correct for her to dance, but this was a private occasion. Besides, Grandmother had not actually forbidden it. Lilac knew herself to be a graceful and spirited dancer who would appear to advantage with the ends of her wide sash floating out as she twirled. Behind her she could hear

Amelia chattering as she and Peter Wentworth took their places in the line.

Alfred's great passions were horses and cards, but before the polka was over he had admitted to himself that Lilac Morton was growing up into a deuced attractive piece. She wasn't enitrely to his taste, there being a faint sharpness to her features that hinted at a will of her own; and her hair hadn't been dressed at all. Still, her eyes were magnificent. Not even the little girl he visited from time to time down in Wandsworth had eyes of so remarkable a tint, shaded by lashes as black and thick as her hair.

"Jolly good." His voice was less languid than usual as the dance spun to its end.

"Yes, indeed. Thank you." The dance had pleased Lilac, and her smile was broad.

"My dear, how delightful that you could come this evening." Mrs Watson rustled up, kissing her warmly on the cheek.

"It's a wonderful party," Lilac said.

"A few friends to welcome Alfred home and wish him godspeed, for it begins to look as if his regiment will be sailing to India quite shortly. How is your dear grandmama?"

"She sends her regards and her thanks for inviting me."

"She would have been most welcome herself," Mrs Watson said graciously, "but her reclusive habits are known to us and respected. She sets us a wonderful example in Christian living."

She wafted the air with her fan as if she were dispersing the odour of sanctity. Amelia's mama looked as Amelia might look in thirty years' time, her plump cheeks sagging, her fair hair dulled to ash. Her gown was of violet taffeta trimmed with black lace, and there were little streaks of perspiration under her arms.

"Wasn't that a splendid polka?" Amelia fluttered up, her face glowing.

"You mustn't get overheated, my love, or you will catch

a chill," her mother warned. "Really, it is not correct for you to be dancing at all, but one cannot deny one's children a little innocent pleasure. Come and talk to Mrs Skelmswood and do remember to ask after Delia."

"What ails Miss Delia Skelmswood?" a voice enquired at Lilac's elbow.

"She is in a decline, Lieutenant Wentworth," Lilac said demurely.

"I am sorry to hear it."

"Oh, it is very sad. She has been in a decline these six years."

The lieutenant gave her a startled look and chuckled. "You have a sly humour," he said. "Is it true you are only just out of school?"

"Out of school, but not out in any other sense of the word," she said ruefully. "If you had sisters you would know that means one is considered too young to require a chaperone at a private function, and far too old to go anywhere in public alone. Too inexperienced to be allowed an opinion on any subject, but far too dangerous to be allowed to dance more than twice even at an informal party."

"Then your second dance must be with me," he said promptly. "Shall it be this next one?"

"My grandmother is not happy about my dancing at all."

"They are playing a gavotte. She can have no objection to a gavotte."

"I have no objection to a gavotte myself, Lieutenant, unless you only dance it with grandmothers."

He offered his arm, his eyes twinkling with merriment. As they began the measure she thought, with a sudden thrill along her nerves, that it was fun to be grown up and make lively conversation and smile. He danced well, never missing the beat of the music, and she hoped that Amelia would appreciate her good fortune when she finally stood at the altar with him.

"You dance beautifully, but it is surely not your only accomplishment?" He looked down at her.

"I fear that it is. My needlework is a disaster, and I am only invited to play the pianoforte when the hostess wishes the guests to go home. By contrast, Amelia's skill with a needle is famous, and she plays very melodiously, accompanying her own singing."

"Then conversation must be your talent. Your words sing in my ears like music."

"You are making fun of me, sir." Her eyes glinted with laughter even while her lips reproached him.

"I hope I would never be so ungallant as to make fun of a lady."

"The dance is ending." She was not sure if she was relieved or sorry.

"And you will not dance again?"

She shook her head, smiling at him.

"I will go and talk with Mrs Skelmswood and ask about Delia."

"Declining Delia," he said, and she choked back laughter as the stately measure ended.

Mrs Skelmswood was only too happy to discuss her daughter's condition, which had baffled doctors for years and might, she was convinced, make medical history. While Lilac listened politely and made the appropriate responses, out of the corner of her eye, she could see the blue skirt floating past. Amelia, however, was dancing with one of her brothers while Lieutenant Wentworth partnered Mavis Adams, who was sweet and gentle and kept missing the step. It was very wrong to feel relief, Lilac scolded herself; but she did.

"And the last physician, a most eminent man, gave it as his considered opinion that the case was completely beyond the resources of present medical knowledge. He told me he had never known a case of galloping consumption to progress so slowly."

"Crawling," Lilac said vaguely, aware that some comment was expected. "Perhaps it is crawling consumption, ma'am."

"I never heard of that. Did your grandmama?"

The dance was ending, and the lieutenant was taking Mavis Adams back to her place. Mrs Watson announced that supper was ready, trying to disguise by the brightness of her tone that her feet hurt and Mr Watson had threatened to retreat to his club if the proceedings didn't liven up.

Lilac continued to feel happy and excited seated between Lieutenant Wentworth and a pallid gentleman who had been invited to make up the numbers. Usually she and Grandmother ate together, and Grandmother liked to hear what Lilac had been doing with herself since the last meal. As Lilac had seldom been doing very much, the conversation generally petered out. Tomorrow, the girl reflected, she would have this evening's activities to talk about. She must remember exactly what the ladies wore and what was served at table. This being a late supper, the hot mushroom consommé was followed by a variety of cold meats, salads, and pâtés with trifle, meringues, cheese, fruit, and a savoury waiting on the sideboard.

"You look exceedingly serious, Miss Morton," the lieutenant said at her elbow. "Do you fear going into a decline?"

"Oh, pray don't." She suppressed a chuckle. "I was merely thinking how pleased Grandmother will be to hear that I had a good time."

"You live with your grandmother?"

"My maternal grandmother reared me. My mother died when I was born, and my father was killed some months before that."

"Killed?" He gave her a questioning look.

"They were missionaries," she explained. "They travelled to America, and he was murdered by savages, after which my mother returned to England."

"Your parents must have been very brave people."

"Yes, indeed. They left me a splendid example." For a

moment she felt slightly gloomy, knowing how difficult it would be for her to live up to that example.

"But you are not planning to enter the mission field?"

"Heavens, no. I shall live with Grandmother until I am married, I suppose, as Amelia will live with her parents." Belatedly Lilac recalled she was supposed to be advancing her friend's cause. "Of course, we hope to continue friends all our lives. Amelia and I have been bosom companions since we were small. When she marries, and such a charming girl is bound to have many suitors, I have promised to be her bridesmaid."

"Or matron-of-honour? When the bridal attendant is herself married is it not called so?"

"It is far more likely that Amelia will be my matron-of-honor. Her husband will be a fortunate man, for she is the dearest girl. She was very popular at school."

"With many accomplishments. I believe you mentioned them."

"And you go to India with your regiment soon? Have you been there before?"

"This will be my first spell of foreign duty. I hope to see some action."

"Not too much action, I trust?"

"There will always be those who don't appreciate the benefits of British rule. However, the southern provinces are very stable, and the social life is most brilliant."

"For someone who has never been to India you have an amazing grasp of the situation," Lilac said solemnly.

"Now you are teasing me, Miss Morton. You do it delightfully."

"Then it is a natural talent," she said on a spurt of laughter, "for it was never on the curriculum at school. You must be looking forward keenly to sailing, though I'm sure your family will miss you."

"With two sons still at home, rather less than I like to believe. However, my father will envy me. I was commissioned into the same regiment from which he was invalided out ten years ago. Now he tries to occupy his days in the administration of the estate and relives his own career in the anticipation of mine."

His tone was amused but affectionate. Lilac guessed there was a deep bond of feeling between him and his father, and that spoke well for the lieutenant's character. Amelia would indeed be fortunate to attract his attention.

"Have you known the Watsons for very long?" She dug her spoon into the trifle the servant had just placed before her.

"I met Alfred when we were in barracks. He was kind enough to invite me to stay when he learned I had no settled place in London."

"Amelia and I have never been out of the city," she said with regret.

"You don't ride?"

"Oh, we trot up and down in the park on fine, summer mornings, but I cannot say that I enjoy it. I would like to break out into a tearing gallop, but that would scandalise everybody. Anyway, I don't keep a horse of my own. I borrow one from the Watson stables, and poor old Diamond would be horrified if I tried to put him to the gallop. Amelia, on the other hand, rides most prettily and receives many compliments though, were you to ask her about it, she would deprecate her skill. She is always apt to think less of herself than she deserves."

"Surely it is a mark of maturity to be aware of one's strengths?"

"But not to boast of them. When you know her better you will find she is most pleasingly modest."

Guiltily aware that she had almost entirely neglected the pale gentleman on her left, she gave a little nod and, turning her head towards him, said politely, "I believe we have not met since the church social last December. Your mother then was not in good health. I do hope she is improved?"

She didn't pay too much attention to the answer, being too conscious of Peter Wentworth's intent blue regard. She wished he would display more interest in Amelia, who was craning her neck at the other end of the table.

The cheese and fruit were being handed round. In a few minutes Frederick would arrive; and Lilac would be whisked away like Cinderella at the Ball, leaving the field to Amelia who was her dearest friend and would make a beautiful, June bride. Lilac stabbed the point of her knife into an unoffending pear and decided fairy tales were stupid.

=3=

"I wonder if I am falling in love?" Lilac asked the question solemnly of her reflection in the mirror and then gave an impatient, little laugh.

It was a ridiculous question, she told herself, because if it needed to be asked then the answer must be in the negative. One surely knew if one were in love or not. She and Amelia had gravely dissected the matter several times and had reached the conclusion that the symptoms of falling in love must include loss of appetite and a tendency to weep when romantic music was played. Lilac had slept soundly and eaten a hearty breakfast, during which she regaled her grandmother with a cheerful account of the previous night's proceedings. Lilac had, however, said very little about Lieutenant Peter Wentworth; and, when she thought of him, she was conscious of a decided fluttering in the region of her heart.

"It won't do you the least particle of good if you are." She addressed the mirror again as severely as if the reflection were a separate person. "Amelia is your dearest friend, and she saw him first. It would be in the highest degree disloyal if you were to sneak in and try to capture his affection for yourself. If you are foolish enough to fall in love, then you must regard it as a sickness from which you will in time recover."

It was useless. The more she pictured the aquiline features, the blue eyes and sweeping cavalry moustache of her supper companion, the warmer grew her cheeks, the more fluttering her heart. Perhaps, it was merely a passing fancy and would die away. She hoped so and resolved never to mention it to Amelia—at least not until they were both elderly matrons. Amelia would have returned from India with her four children by then, her skin a trifle yellowed from the sun; and she and Lilac would enjoy a comfortable gossip together.

"You know, years ago, I had quite a tendresse for your husband," Lilac would say airily. "It was quite absurd, but I envied you dreadfully until I met my own dear whatever his name turns out to be."

Lilac jumped at a tap on the door.

Alice opened the door and put her mobcapped head round it. "Miss Lilac, there's a gentleman downstairs."

"Then tell Grandmother."

"If you please, the gentleman's called to see you, and Mrs Barbara went to see the vicar about the bazaar for the new church organ."

"That's right. I forgot." Lilac had excused herself from the visit to the vicar on the pretext of having to write a thank you note to Mrs Watson.

"He did say as he wishes to see you," Alice repeated helpfully.

"I'll come down." Struck by a thought, Lilac hesitated, then continued. "Did he give his name?"

"Lieutenant Wentworth, miss. Ever so handsome he is," Alice said, bridling a little.

"He's a friend of Amelia's. Make some coffee and take it to him in the morning room. I'll be down directly."

"Yes, Miss Lilac." The head withdrew, and the door closed.

Lilac stared at herself. The reflection in the mirror had pink cheeks and sparkling eyes. She was annoyed that she had put on one of her older dresses, a brown merino with full sleeves patterned in lemon and a paler brown. It had been an attractive dress when she first had it made a couple of years before, but now it looked drab and schoolgirlish.

Well, it would be foolish to change. The lieutenant was probably coming to thank her for having pointed him in Amelia's direction. He would have talked to Amelia after Lilac's departure and seen for himself her real sweetness. Maybe she had played the pianoforte.

Lilac pushed back her heavy tail of hair and went sedately down the stairs into the morning room that overlooked the narrow garden at the back. Peter Wentworth jumped up from the chair on which he was perched somewhat gingerly and bowed.

"Miss Morton, good morning." He sounded as if the morning had only become good as she entered the room. "I trust you slept well?"

"Very well."

She motioned him back to the chair and seated herself at a little distance. This was the first time in her life she had ever had a gentleman caller, but she hoped she could carry off the situation as if it were a common occurrence.

"You were not fatigued after the supper, I hope. I did not have the opportunity of bidding you good-night."

"Frederick doesn't like to keep the horses waiting, and I was not in the least tired. I'd be a poor sort of creature if two dances and a bite of supper wore me out."

"I think you are a splendid creature," he exclaimed. Then displayed how young he was by flushing scarlet.

"That's very kind of you, Lieutenant." She made the expected response, feeling her own cheeks begin to burn. "It is also kind of you to call. My grandmother is out unfortunately, but she will be back very soon. She is always interested in meeting friends of—Amelia's and my friends. Meanwhile, may I offer you coffee? Here is Alice with the tray. Or would you prefer something else?"

At school, they had held mock tea parties with the girls taking turns at being the gentleman callers. Lilac vaguely recalled Miss Stevenson informing them that gentlemen frequently preferred something stronger.

"Coffee will be splendid, Miss Morton," he assured her as Alice put the tray on the table and bobbed out.

"We have milk and sugar." She poured carefully, irritated by the fussy gestures her hands were making. "There are biscuits too."

"A splash of milk and two lumps of sugar, if I may?"

"There." She concentrated on the small task as intently as if she were launching a ship. When she handed him the cup their fingers touched briefly, and she was aware of her heart beating very fast again.

"There is nothing like a good cup of coffee," he said.

"Unless it is two cups of coffee," she said foolishly and wondered what had happened to all the wit and vivacity she had displayed the previous evening. Alone with him she was behaving like a complete idiot. At least he would not be tempted to admire her more than Amelia. She wished she could take more comfort in this reflection.

"I beg your pardon?" He had said something she had completely missed.

"I asked if you would do me the honour of riding with me one day this week. I am sure I can find you a more spirited horse than the sluggish Diamond."

"Riding? No, I couldn't possibly. At least . . . you are inviting me to join you in a—a party, is that it? You and Alfred and Amelia."

"I thought we could ride alone. With the grooms in attendance, of course."

"I couldn't," she repeated. "My grandmother would never allow it."

"Then I shall not be too downcast," he said, "since your refusal proceeds from the knowledge of your grandmother's prohibition rather than your own unwillingness. I hope I have not offended you by asking?"

"No indeed. It is only that . . . it would be much more suitable if you asked Amelia. She has the most charming air on horseback."

"But would it not be equally improper to ask her?" he enquired.

"Not when you are a friend of Alfred's and a guest in the Watson home."

"Do you think your grandmother might be induced to invite me here as a guest?" he asked solemnly.

"It wouldn't be any use. I have no brother named Alfred."

Catching each other's glance they burst out laughing simultaneously.

"Etiquette tyrannises over us all," he said wryly. "I fear I am not strong enough to rebel, but it would be agreeable to flout convention and behave as fancy takes us, would it not?"

"It would be exciting, but we are neither of us likely to do it." Lilac hesitated, then said with an air deliberately casual, "If, however, a party was to be got up, then I am certain that Grandmother would allow me to ride; but you must not think of choosing a mount for me. I always borrow Diamond."

"Perhaps it will be possible to arrange something. The truth is that we are embarking for India sooner than anyone expected. We sail at the end of the month," he said. "Miss Morton, are your affections engaged anywhere?"

"Lieutenant Wentworth!" Lilac realised she was staring at him with her mouth open. She pressed her lips hastily together.

"I have approached everything in the wrong manner," he said contritely. "I merely wished to be assured that any future visits I made would not interfere with any previous attachments you may have formed."

In a moment he would be proposing, and she would be accepting. It was all too soon. It was all far too soon.

"I hope we may become friends during the short time you are here," she said at last. "I . . . that is Amelia and I . . ."

Lilac hadn't the faintest idea what she wanted to say

about Amelia and herself but fortunately was spared having to complete the sentence by the sound of the front door and her grandmother's voice in the hall. A moment later Barbara Lameter's plump, black-clad figure was in the room, her eyes questioning above her smiling lips.

"Grandmother, this is Lieutenant Peter Wentworth, Alfred's friend," Lilac said hastily.

"Lieutenant Wentworth, how d'ye do?" Shaking hands, Barbara inspected him.

"Lieutenant Wentworth called to pay his respects to you," Lilac said.

"That was very civil of you." Barbara frowned slightly. "Wentworth? Your grandfather would not have been Colonel George Wentworth, by any chance?"

"Yes, ma'am."

"And you are making the Army your career too? I have a great respect for tradition. You will be going to India with your regiment?"

"Yes, ma'am. We've received warning it will probably be at the end of the month."

"The lieutenant hoped to persuade me to join a riding party, if one can be arranged before he leaves," Lilac put in. "Alfred and Amelia—"

"If the Watsons invite you there is no reason why you cannot accept," Barbara said. "It is most civil of Lieutenant Wentworth to bring you the news. I am happy to have met you. I see that Lilac has given you some refreshment."

"And I repaid her by taking up far too much of her time, and yours, ma'am." He was on his feet, bowing. "I hope to have the pleasure of calling on you again."

"Colonel Wentworth's grandson will be most welcome."

He shot a look full of things unspoken in Lilac's direction, then was gone, leaving a space in the room.

"That's a very amiable young man," her grandmother commented. "You mentioned him as having been at the supper party last night, but I hadn't realised you had become such good friends so quickly."

"He is looking for a wife," Lilac said incautiously.

"My dear girl, I trust he didn't make his purpose known in so crass a manner," Barbara said.

"No, of course not." Lilac flushed. "It is only that the young officers are encouraged to take wives in order to settle them down."

"One should marry for more than the wish to oblige one's commanding officer," Barbara said dryly.

"And if one falls in love? What if one falls in love . . . suddenly?"

"Five minutes out of school and the child talks of falling in love." The other spoke lightly, but there was a shadow in her eyes.

"Mama was only seventeen when she fell in love with Papa," Lilac argued.

"The case was unusual. Your mama was very mature and thoughtful for her age, more interested in things of the spirit; and your papa was past thirty. I felt that I could safely trust her to him and—this is a very foolish conversation," said Barbara breaking off abruptly. "You only met the young gentleman last night, and he is going to India very soon. You are not going to try to convince me that you have fallen in love or some such nonsense, have you?"

"I am not certain how I feel." Lilac's eyes met the eyes of the older woman with frank appeal. "Amelia gave me to understand that she liked him herself. But he was most attentive at supper though I did keep directing the conversation back to Amelia, and this morning he called and he hinted—"

"On the basis of a light flirtation and a few hints you are going to build a love affair? You are very young and silly, Lilac. Why, if you sigh over every handsome young man you meet you will begin to acquire a reputation for being shallow and foolish. I am a trifle disappointed in you, my love, especially since you know that Amelia is not indifferent to him and he is a guest in her father's house."

Barbara spoke with severity, and Lilac's heart sank.

Perhaps it was foolish of her to pay attention to what might be only the gallantries of a practised flirt, but she found that difficult to believe. Peter Wentworth had an openness and an honesty about him that she felt was sincere.

"He has not said anything in the least unbecoming to a gentleman," she protested.

"My dear, I am sure he has not. He comes from an old and honourable family," Barbara said more gently. "His grandfather died a hero. He follows in noble footsteps and it is only natural that he should be taken with you for you are growing into a very pretty girl, though you must take care not to become vain. You must learn to look before you leap."

"I shall look twice," Lilac declared, her high spirits bubbling up again.

She sketched a curtsy to her grandmother that had in it all the loving impertinence of youth and went out. Barbara Lameter sat down on the chair her granddaughter had just vacated and untied the strings of her bonnet slowly. Lilac was seventeen and growing into a greater beauty than Mary· had ever been. There was a vibrancy and spirit in her face the gentler Mary had lacked.

"You can't expect to keep the secret forever," Philip had said during his last visit. "If the chit wants to get married—"

"I will deal with that when the moment arrives," Barbara had interrupted.

Now, seated in her morning room, she wondered if the moment had already come. Lilac couldn't be kept a child forever. Sooner or later she would fall in love, and then the telling could no longer be delayed. The man who wished to marry her must be informed, in the strictest confidence, of course, about her background. If he accepted it, then his would be the responsibility to tell Lilac as much as he deemed necessary for her to know. A terrible shock to her, no doubt, but the shock would be cushioned by his loving assurance that her circumstances made no difference to his feelings. There was no denying that a marriage with Peter Wentworth would be an excellent match. If the young man could accept the truth. Barbara frowned, rubbing her left arm which had begun to ache again. She must tell Alice to make the hot poultice which sometimes relieved this recurring discomfort.

Meanwhile, Lilac, too restless to remain quietly within doors, had flitted into the stable yard which was separated by a high wall from the garden. The two elderly carriage horses greeted her with pleasure, advancing their noses beyond their stalls in hopes of sugar. Lilac patted them absently. She was thinking about the lieutenant who, under the stimulus of imminent departure, had almost made a declaration. She was also thinking of Amelia, who would be terribly hurt and of her grandmother who, like all old people, couldn't avoid a certain resentment at the younger folk growing up. Of herself, Lilac didn't think too deeply. It was sufficient for her that, at this wonderful moment, she existed, standing in the warm stable with the horses nuzzling her and the memory of blue eyes in a handsome face crystal clear in her mind.

Unfortunately, Amelia herself came round later in the day. She packed her attendant maid off to drink coffee with Alice in the kitchen, expressed polite regret that Mrs Lameter was resting, then drew Lilac into the drawing room and scarcely awaited the closing of the door before she embarked on breathless confidences.

"I could not get away until now for Mama always has the megrim after a party and requires endless attention. What was your opinion of him? Isn't he as handsome as I said? He told me that he had called here this morning to pay his respects to Mrs Lameter who knew his grandfather, but you will know that already of course. Did he talk of me at all? I was longing to hear what he way saying to you last night, but I was too far down the table. Originally Mama had placed me next to him, but I considered it would be more subtle to have him seated next to you. Did he express any opinion?"

"Not directly," Lilac said cautiously. "It would not have been very well-mannered of him to have done so when he is a guest in your parents' house. I spoke of you very warmly, and he nodded his head and appeared most interested."

"There is a positive rash of engagements among the officers," Amelia said. "Mama professes to be shocked, but she would love to be planning a wedding herself."

"You would miss your season."

"Which would please Papa, who is forever grumbling that he will be a beggar by the time he has brought us all out. It is becoming quite á la mode to catch a husband before one's season, and there is rumour of Peter's father being in the running for a knighthood."

"You call him Peter?"

"Not to his face. Not yet." Amelia blushed. "I think it possible that I may call him so very soon, though. After you went home he prevailed upon Mama to allow me to dance for a third time, and he said how much he was enjoying his visit."

"Perhaps we ought not to attach too much importance to his being polite," Lilac began, but Amelia interrupted her gaily.

"What an old sobersides you are. Dearest Lilac, you are so good-hearted that the prospect of my being disappointed terrifies you. I promise that soon you will be wishing me happiness."

"I do that already," said Lilac.

She was beginning to feel utterly wretched. For the first time in their friendship she longed for Amelia to bring the visit to an end, but she stayed on and only tore herself away after she had extracted a promise from Lilac to come to tea at the Watsons the following day.

"If the weather continues fine we hope to have it in the garden. Alfred is anxious that you should come. He was very taken with you last night. Said you were a deuced fine girl. From Aflred that is high praise indeed, usually reserved for a racehorse. Wouldn't it be too delicious if you and I had a double wedding?"

Lilac smiled weakly, and Amelia took herself off in innocent good humour. Soon after, Grandmother awoke in a cross mood because her rheumatism was paining her. The evening dragged on. Lilac took a book and pretended to bury herself in it. There was nothing unusual in that. She had always been fond of reading, but tonight her eyes skimmed the page without taking in the sense of the words while her mind lost itself in dreaming.

"Mrs Peter Wentworth. Lilac Wentworth." It sounded right. She wondered if her mother had sat, silently changing her name from Lameter to Morton. She wished her mother was here to confide in.

=4=

AT THE BEGINNING of the week Lilac had suspected herself of being in love. By the end of the week she was almost certain of it. When she thought of the lieutenant she found herself in a state of trembling eagerness, and she had begun to think of him most of the time. On the appointed day she went to the Watsons for tea, afraid she might be disappointed when she saw him again, even more afraid he might find her less attractive than he had supposed. She had driven Alice nearly crazy by demanding her services for two full hours and by discarding one dress after another until the floor was heaped with petticoats and Alice was impelled to exclaim, "Lawks, Miss. Anybody would think you was going to tea with the Prince Regent."

In the end Lilac decided on a gown of green taffeta, its skirt patterned with sprigs of pink flowers. Pointed collar and cuffs of lace gave the dress a pristine air, and a straw bonnet with pink and green ribbons completed the ensemble. Alice had done her best with Lilac's heavy hair, pinning it at the nape of her neck in a chignon which they both agreed made her look at least nineteen.

It was a pity there were only six streets between the two houses since Lilac had scarcely stepped grandly into the carriage and settled herself before she was stepping out again and being greeted by Mrs Watson.

"The young people are all in the garden, my dear. You know the way."

Mrs Watson never ventured her own nose into the sunlight

unless shielded by a thick veil and a parasol. She watched Lilac skim down the hall towards the French windows.

"My clothes are all wrong," was her first dismayed reaction.

The other girls wore pale muslins and light cottons, and there were sunshades fixed to the wicker chairs. She hesitated, raising her hand to her eyes. She looked like an exotic bird alighted amid a flock of doves. One of the doves fluttered to her side.

"There you are. I had quite given you up. We have cucumber salad and peach preserves and three kinds of cake so we are not likely to starve. We are going to play croquet and I shall be exceedingly put out if I don't win."

There were half a dozen young officers present, but Lilac had picked him out at once and knew in that instant she was not going to revise her first impression of him. Neither, it seemed, was he; for, though he only bowed politely and enquired after her grandmother, his eyes lingered on her so warmly that she dreaded Amelia might notice.

Fortunately, Amelia was too busy playing hostess, ordering the young gentlemen to pass round the refreshments and tossing her ringlets to display her vivacity. The other girls had been schoolmates of theirs. Two of them were already engaged so there was a great deal of teasing and laughter. Lilac teased and laughed with the rest, but all the time a part of her stood aside, observing everything from a distance, thinking that nobody was saying anything that really mattered, and that Amelia tossed her curls a little too frequently.

"You look a trifle pale, Miss Morton. Is the heat enervating?" Peter Wentworth was addressing her.

"No indeed." She jerked her attention back. "I love the sun and horrify my grandmother because I tan so easily. She considers it most unladylike."

"I don't believe you could do anything unladylike." He added in a lower tone, "Is it not possible for us to speak alone?"

"Not here, not anywhere if we are to avoid giving offence." Her tone was equally low. Then Amelia called that the hoops were set up, and Alfred came to claim her as his partner.

They played croquet though afterwards she couldn't remember who had won. She forgot that her dress had seemed too bright and, instead, felt special somehow, like a flower reaching for the sun. It had not even mattered that Frederick came to collect her before she had spoken to the lieutenant again. She was in that stage of loving when the company of the beloved is not absolutely essential and it is almost sufficient to dream.

That evening, reading a volume of poetry which had been her graduation prize from school, she was struck by the fact that so many of the poems were about lost and tragic loves. Very few poets had taken pleasure in their loving. Perhaps happy lovers didn't need to write things down. Yet she would have liked to express something of what she felt in lasting form.

Below her window a footfall sounded in the quiet street. She raised the curtain a fraction and saw the lamplight gleaming on a blond head. Then he looked up, sketched a salute and stood there until she let the curtain fall back into place.

The next morning he was at church in the Watsons' pew with Amelia next to him, wearing her new bonnet with the yellow streamers and looking good enough to eat. Still, Peter Wentworth kept glancing towards the Lameter pew. Catching his eye, Lilac looked down hastily at her prayer book and wished she had worn something more exciting than her grey pelisse. Afterwards there were the usual greetings exchanged with Mrs Watson's voice louder than the rest.

"So delightful to have dear Lilac's company. I am never more in my element than when I have young people about me, though my brood grows smaller."

"Lilac is happy to receive your invitations. I only wish it

were possible . . ." Barbara made a sad little gesture with her hands.

But it is possible, Lilac thought suddenly. It is seventeen years since Mama died. There is no reason for Grandmother to wear black still and never entertain. She was a little shocked at her own impatience as if something cold and critcial had entered her. Then Peter Wentworth was bowing to her.

"You look very lovely, Miss Morton. I found it hard to concentrate on the service."

"Oh, pray hush." She put up her hand to catch at her bonnet as a sudden gust of wind tugged at the strings. "I would feel terribly guilty if I imagined I had diverted you from your worship."

"You were absorbed in the sermon, I suppose?"

"Riveted," she said, and chuckled, happy to be talking to him.

"Miss Lilac, if I may call you so? I wish you to know that . . . ."

"Your grandmama's looking capital this morning, if I may say so. Wonderful how some ladies seem to get younger as they get older." Alfred had strolled up and taken her arm with the ease of an old acquaintance. She glanced regretfully towards Peter Wentworth, but he had moved away and was escorting her grandmother down the path to Frederick and the waiting carriage.

"And some babies look elderly, I suppose," Lilac said.

"Ah, quite so. That is deuced good. I must remember that. Elderly babies."

"What are you two laughing about?" Amelia enquired, escaping from the vicar who had been trying to persuade her to take a stall at the forthcoming bazaar.

"Lilac—I suppose I ought to say Miss Lilac now—made a capital jest about elderly babies. Must try to remember it."

"Alfred, go and talk to Mrs Dakers. You know her son wishes to join your regiment, and she is hoping you will put in a good word with your colonel." Amelia took her friend's arm and walked with her down the path. "Alfred is such a fool, but a perfect dear and absolutely *silly* about you. Lieutenant Wentworth informed us last night that he has quite made up his mind to marry if the lady will have him. Those were his exact words, spoken in a most feeling tone. I said I was sure that she would and he went very red and looked at his boots."

As well he might, Lilac thought with a spasm of rueful amusement. He must realise that Amelia has a tendresse for him, and he is staying with the family.

"He seems a very agreeable gentleman," she said.

"I want you so much to like him," Amelia said fervently. "I have such a high regard for your opinion that I do declare I might be tempted to refuse him if you disapproved."

This was becoming intolerable.

"Grandmother is waiting," said Lilac in some confusion. "I had better join her. I do wish you well, Amelia, truly I do." Amelia squeezed her arm by way of reply and turned back towards her family. Seating herself next to Barbara, Lilac had the suspicion that soon Amelia would no longer be her bosom friend, but she could see no way of avoiding the inevitable breach. Lilac sat in silence, glad that her companion had drawn her veil over her face and seemed disposed to sit in silence too.

Sunday was always a dull day. After the midday meal, which was always roast beef, the afternoon was a sluggish time when Barbara received and paid few calls. Lilac usually fidgeted between the house and the garden wondering why a holy day had to be so tedious. Today, however, Grandmother unexpectedly asked her to visit the Smiths.

"Poor Mrs Smith had her latest six weeks ago and I have not taken her anything. I feel most guilty about it."

It was odd that Grandmother's guilt could only be assuaged by sending Lilac out on a long walk, since after church the horses were always rested.

"I would go myself." She interpreted her granddaughter's expression correctly. "But this heat would quite overpower me, and you were saying only the other week that you found Sundays tedious. Alice's sister lives near the Smiths so she can accomany you and visit there while you are with Mrs Smith."

Occasional visits to people like the Smiths, who were respectable but in straightened circumstances, constituted good words. Lilac had sometimes gone with Barbara to some family designated by the vicar as a deserving case, but had always felt as if she were intruding into another world. The Smiths, however, were lively and cheerful, from Bert who had lost an arm at Trafalgar, to Eliza, a two-year-old bundle of mischief.

After the meal Lilac and Alice set out, both carrying large baskets with a selection of what Cook called "eatables and wearables." As the afternoon promised to be hot Lilac donned her straw bonnet and a light pelisse and half hoped they might meet the lieutenant out for a stroll, since the pelisse was almost the same shade as her eyes and suited her beautifully. They met nobody who was in the slightest degree interesting, however; and, long before they reached the tiny rented house into which a family of nine squeezed, her feet were aching abominably.

The reception sweetened her temper, for Mrs Smith was a pleasant, little woman with a fund of amusing stories about the scrapes into which her lively brood tumbled. Meanwhile, the children stared openmouthed at Lilac as if she were a princess dropped from a fairy tale. There was the new baby to be admired, and the contents of the baskets to be unpacked and exclaimed over. Algy must recite the poem with gestures he'd learned, and by the time Lilac rose to go she was glad she had come. She had been told often how much her mother enjoyed visiting the poor and had always felt ashamed that she was not keener on doing the same. Now her conscience was agreeably light as she walked back with Alice through the quiet Sunday streets.

"I must visit the Smiths more often," said Lilac. "Little Edward is so sweet."

"And next year there'll be another baby more than likely," Alice said. "You'd think they'd 'ave more sense."

"I don't see what sense has to do with having babies," Lilac said, puzzled. "Grandmother says they are gifts from the Lord."

"And He's a heap more generous to the poor when it comes to sending babies," Alice said wryly as they went up the steps.

Barbara was up, a tray of tea and scones at her side, her black lace cap on her head. She looked tired, as if she hadn't had her sleep out properly. Pausing in the doorway, Lilac was struck by the fact that her grandmother was old. Lilac went to her side. "Did you miss me while you were taking your nap?" she said in her quick, warm voice. "We had a splendid visit, and Mrs Smith was so grateful for the clothes and the jam and spiced ham and pound cake. She asked after you most respectfully, and the new baby is so sweet. He scarcely has time to cry, there being so many to nurse him."

"You're a good girl to have gone," Barbara said. Her voice sounded flat and dull, the way it sometimes did when they talked of Mama, and Grandmother relived the pain of her loss all over again. Perhaps she was ill.

"Don't you feel well, Grandmother?" Lilac regarded her with concern.

"The pain in my arm has been troubling me. I may ask Doctor Sims to look at it if it doesn't improve. Tell me about the Smith baby."

Lilac related the details of her visit though she had the feeling her grandmother was listening with only half an ear. Perhaps it had been thoughtless of her to chatter so freely about falling in love, since it must inevitably have turned the older woman's mind to thoughts of their eventual parting. For the rest of the day Lilac was careful not to mention the subject and confined her conversation to less sensitive topics such as the forthcoming bazaar.

When they retired for the night she resisted the temptation to lift her bedroom curtain. It was not very ladylike to make so plain that she was watching out for him. Besides, there was a delicious uncertainty about imagining him below, waiting patiently in hope of catching sight of her. The next morning the hot weather had broken. Rain pattered on the sills and filled the gutters. Not until mid-afternoon did it cease and a reluctant sun gleam briefly through the scudding clouds. Lilac was debating whether or not to risk a short walk in the garden when the Watson carriage drew up and Amelia alighted, clutching her cloak round her as she hurried up the steps.

"Lilac, I was praying you would not have ventured out, for you must positively be the very first to know," bubbled Amelia, catching at her friend's hands as they met in the hallway. "I could not endure to keep it to myself even though it is to be made official in the next day or two, as soon as permission is obtained from the commanding officer. Lieutenant Wentworth spoke to Papa last evening, and this morning he paid his addresses to me."

Lilac had been taken to a fair once where there were swing boats that tilted up very high, then brought one down in a rush. She had that exact same sensation now as she heard Amelia's words.

"Of course, Mama cried a little for the wedding will be very soon, but she will have Sophie to bring out in a year or two, so she is really not too upset. Peter—I may call him that now—must sail with his regiment, but I shall follow on the next passenger ship. Fortunately we had begun on my wardrobe for the Season, so now it will do duty as a trousseau, though I'll not need so many warm things, and everything will be a mite hurried. Oh, do say you are happy for me."

"We are both very happy for you, my dear," Barbara Lameter, emerging from the morning room, spoke steadily.

"It is also a great surprise. You have scarcely met the young gentleman."

"That was what Papa said," Amelia dimpled. "He wished at first for an unofficial betrothal, but Lieutenant Wentworth was importunate. After all, this is eighteen-seventeen and not the dark ages. So he was persuaded to agree and I have been in seventh heaven and longing for the rain to ease off, so that I could come and tell you. There is to be a small party the day after tomorrow, just for close friends, and you as my closest friend will be the guest of honour, Lilac. I swear it's due to your good offices that I'm to be married at all."

"I shall be delighted to come," Lilac said. She was astonished to hear the words emerging easily, the same as if there were no yawning gulf at her feet.

"I don't suppose I could prevail upon you to come, Mrs Lameter? I know you don't usually."

"I think for this occasion I will break my rule," Barbara said with a smile. "It is such exciting news that Lilac and I are rendered almost dumb. We have not offered you refreshment or even invited you to sit down. Lilac, ring for Alice."

"Oh, I can't stay above a moment," Amelia said. "Mama is drawing up the guest list, and the invitations must be despatched immediately. She was quite sharp with me when I insisted on coming out."

"Then we'll not keep you, my dear. Convey our felicitations to Lieutenant Wentworth, and tell your mama we shall be delighted to attend your engagement party."

"Yes, indeed," said Lilac.

"You will be my bridesmaid? On that I am determined," Amelia said, kissing her. Then she had left, wafting down the rainwashed steps, taking all Lilac's hopes with her.

"There has to be a mistake," Lilac said aloud. "Lieutenant Wentworth made it so very clear—."

"Are you telling me he actually proposed to you?" her grandmother demanded.

"No. He would have come first to you to ask leave, but he made his intentions so very clear, Grandmother. He fixed on me from the first."

"Fixed on you for a little light flirtation perhaps. Well—"

"It was more than that," Lilac interrupted, her voice shaking. "There was an instant, mutual attraction."

"Which on his part seems to have been of remarkably short duration," Barbara said dryly. "You must accept the situation and try to make the best of it. After so brief an acquaintanceship your feelings cannot have been deeply involved."

She spoke calmly, as if a broken heart were a matter as trivial as a sprained ankle. Lilac felt a dull resentment colouring her misery. The trouble was that Grandmother was too old, nearly sixty, and long past remembering what it was like to love a man.

"I cannot possibly go to the party," said Lilac. "It would be too humiliating."

"Humiliating for whom? No promise has been made or broken. The young man did not behave well in seeming to seek you out, but that is no reason for your behaving as if you had been jilted. Amelia is your best friend, and it is your duty to be happy for her."

"I would," Lilac burst out, "if she were marrying somebody else."

"A very selfish, ill-considered remark. I hoped to find you more mature in your attitude. Certainly I expected more pride. How could you possibly explain away your absence at your best friend's engagement celebration?"

"You don't understand," Lilac said. There were mutinous tears in her eyes, and her hands were clenched tightly together. "Oh, you don't understand."

She could not possibly have mistaken his interest in her, the manner in which he pressed her hand at meeting and parting. He had stood musing beneath her window. He hadn't been thinking of proposing to Amelia then. Perhaps he mistook her shyness for indifference. If she were to find him and explain—but she could not possibly do anything so improper. At least she had that much pride. Pride seemed to be all Lilac had as she went slowly up the stairs to her room and slumped down on the end of the bed. Her face contorted with the pain of the raw space where her heart had been.

Barbara stood for a few minutes in the hall, listening to her granddaughter's footsteps along the upper landing. Then the opening and closing of the bedroom door. Barbara turned and walked stiffly into the parlour. She wanted to weep, but it was years since she had permitted herself that luxury. She cried bitterly when Mary had died then dried her tears and set herself to the task of rearing of Mary's child.

If only Lieutenant Wentworth had been the right man, but he had proved he was not. She would never forget the stunned expression on his handsome, young face when she told him the story. He made some stumbling remark about having to think it over and left just in time before Lilac returned from her visit to the Smiths. Barbara was only grateful he had announced his intention of calling as he handed her up to the carriage after church. She knew he wouldn't come back again, but she had not expected him to burn his boots so thoroughly. Barbara Lameter closed her eyes briefly, feeling the nag of pain intensify in her arm. She was not going to weep, she told herself fiercely, and held her breath against the gathering agony as it crept into her ribs.

=5=

THE SUDDEN DEATH of Barbara Lameter, though devastating to Lilac, was scarcely felt in the world at large. She had lived so quietly that her going caused barely a ripple.

"If she had come to me six months ago I would have recommended some precautions to stave off such a massive attack," Doctor Sims told Lilac regretfully. "However, I doubt if it would have been of much use. She enjoyed her food too well and never took sufficient exercise."

"Could shock have caused it?" Lilac asked calmly, too calmly in the doctor's opinion.

"Had she received some kind of shock?"

"No, no. I merely wondered." The palms of her hands were hot and sticky. She rubbed them down the side of her skirt and thought, *I will feel better when I have taken a bath and drunk something cool.*

"With regard to the arrangements . . ." The doctor looked at her.

"Arrangements? Oh, yes. The funeral." She had forgotten about that. "Will the undertaker see to that? I am not familiar—"

"I will sign the certificate and register it for you, and I will call in at the vicarage and the funeral parlour," he said reassuringly. "Is there nobody who can stay with you?"

"There's Uncle Philip, but we've not seen him for years. He's in Africa, I think." She frowned. "I really think I can contrive with Cook and Alice and Mr Briggs and Frederick.

Oh, the solicitor should be informed. I'll have someone take a note round to him at once."

"And then may I recommend some sleep? It is the best antidote to grief. Take one of these tablets with a cup of tea. You are not nervous to be in the house?"

"Nervous?" Lilac looked at him blankly, then shook her head. "No, I'm not nervous."

"The undertaker will be here first thing in the morning." Doctor Sims patted her shoulder and went out.

And the vicar and Mr Benjamin Green, the lawyer, Lilac thought bleakly. It will be quite a party.

Of course, she would not now be going to the other party, and her mourning would serve as excuse for not attending the wedding. It was ironic that Grandmother had to die to save Lilac from watching Peter Wentworth marry Amelia. Lilac prayed he would not come to offer condolences while, at the same time, another part of her wished he would arrive at the door any moment now to tell her it had all been a grotesque mistake and she was the one he loved after all. She ate the soup that Cook sent up and took the pill Doctor Sims had left. It made her so heavy-eyed she could hardly keep awake long enough to take off her clothes.

Modest though the funeral was it still entailed a great deal of running to and fro. The undertaker was there with his two assistants. Also the vicar, ladies from the Church Aid Society, the few neighbours with whom Barbara Lameter had been on visiting terms, Mrs Smith, who had left the new baby at home and come to press Lilac's hands in inarticulate sympathy, and, of course, the Watsons.

Lilac had dreaded the Watsons coming to condole, but it was easier than she had expected. Amelia wept and kissed her. Mrs Watson invited Lilac to stay with them and was only prevented from insisting by the assurance that Uncle Philip might arrive soon. Lilac had despatched a message to him at his last known address. In reality, it might be months before he turned up. However, she had kept that information to herself, taking the visitors into the parlour where Grandmother lay, not looking like herself at all but like a waxen figure who had nothing to do with the hushed bustle going on around.

I wish she hadn't died just when she did, Lilac thought over and over.

It could have happened at any time. Doctor Sims had been definite about that. Lilac wished her last words to her grandmother hadn't been a reproach. She wished she could be certain that the news of Amelia's betrothal hadn't provided the final shock.

"Peter was very sorry indeed to hear the sad news," Amelia said when they were in the hall. "He sends his regrets. The party really ought to be postponed out of respect for an old friend, but as it now appears definite they are sailing at the end of the month—"

"Lilac wouldn't expect you to, my dear," her mother broke in.

"No, of course not. You must continue with the arrangements you have made," Lilac said.

"And you are positive you will be all right?" Amelia's pretty face was full of concern.

I must remember that none of this is her fault, Lilac thought.

"We will naturally be at the funeral." Mrs Watson embraced Lilac in her turn. "If you require any help you know where to come."

She, too, was sincere in her sympathy, but Lilac found it impossible to forget that they were hurrying away to write wedding invitations while, for herself, there was no respite from the business of mourning. She already had a black dress. One never knew when it might be required, Barbara had said in answer to her granddaughter's objection that it was a dismal garment. Barbara had not suspected, of course, that it would be worn for her. Lilac wished she had not cried so much after she heard of Amelia's engagement because now all her tears seemed to be dried up, leaving nothing but a dull, heavy ache.

There was a curious unreality about the funeral. Mr Benjamin Green, who exactly suited the layman's idea of a lawyer, accompanied her in the carriage, patting her hand occasionally and helping her in and out as tenderly as if she were an invalid. There were half a dozen other carriages at the churchyard, including the Watsons, but a quick glance told her the lieutenant had not come. Amelia wept a little, but it was no more than an April rainstorm. Her wedding was too near for her to be more than briefly unhappy, and Lilac could not help noticing that, as the mourners left the graveyard, Amelia took off her gloves, and on her left hand was a diamond ring.

She wishes me to be happy for her, Lilac thought, forcing herself to smile as she gave a small nod to indicate she had seen the ring.

It was not Amelia's fault. Neither was it her fault that her whispered, "Dearest Lilac, it will not be the same without you as my bridesmaid," gave the other a pang of grief worse than any she had known since she had found her grandmother crumpled on the parlour floor. Mr Green touched Lilac's arm, and they walked back to the carriage where Frederick waited with crepe festooning his hat. There would not be the customary funeral tea. Lilac was the sole relative, and Barbara Lameter had made no intimate friendships. There was the will to be read, but Mr Green had already intimated that it was a simple document, necessitating only the presence of Lilac and the servants.

"A sad occasion," he said. "Mrs Lameter was a good woman, a gentlewoman, a sterling example of good breeding and gentility. May I say how very impressed I was by your bearing during this ordeal? And it must surely have been such for so young a lady."

Lilac said nothing. She felt she could claim little credit for her fortitude. In the parlour she took a high-backed chair as the servants filed in. Mr Green, the will on the table before him, cleared his throat slightly to gain their undivided attention.

"Mrs Lameter made her will five years ago and has not added or altered anything in any way since," he informed them. "It is a straightforward document which, when shorn of its legal terminology, provides as follows: 'I leave the sum of fifty pounds each to every member of the staff who has been in service here for more than five years at the time of my decease, together with separate character references should any of them wish to seek a new position.' I have the references here, signed by Mrs Lameter."

"Does that mean we 'ave to leave?" Cook asked.

"That will be for Mr Philip Lameter to decide when he returns," the lawyer said. "The rest of the will concerns Miss Morton only, so you are free to leave."

"Fifty pounds is very nice, very nice indeed," Cook remarked as they filed out. "I always said as Mrs Lameter would see us right."

"Is anything wrong?" Lilac sat up a little straighter.

"Not at all, Miss Morton," Mr Green hastened to assure her. "I merely considered it unnecessary to acquaint the domestics with the precise situation since it does not affect them. Your grandmother continues thus." He ran his index finger down the document and read aloud, " 'As my late husband's estate was willed entirely to Mr. Philip Lameter as a mark of his displeasure at my failure to have a son, I have only my personal effects and my affection to leave to my granddaughter, Lilac Mary Morton, together with the sum of one thousand pounds less the bequests to the servants. I am confident that, should my death occur before her marriage, my brother-in-law will continue to extend to her the support he has so kindly extended to me.' "

"Then I go on living here?" Lilac looked at him questioningly.

"I am certain that when Mr Philip Lameter arrives he will agree that you should continue to regard this as your home," he assured her. "Of course, you cannot possibly remain here alone. However, a suitable chaperone will, I am sure, be found."

"And the money?" the moment she had asked she feared it sounded mercernary.

Mr Green replied promptly, nonetheless. "The will has to be probated, but that will take only a short time. There are the bequests to the servants to be deducted leaving eight hundred pounds. If you require an advance I can arrange it."

"I would like three hundred pounds, and I would like you to invest the remaining five hundred for me," Lilac said promptly.

"Three hundred pounds is a lot of money," he began doubtfully.

"It will give me a feeling of independence." She rose, small and slim in her black gown and held out her hand. "Thank you for all your help and advice. I hope I may consult you if it is ever necessary?"

"My door is always open, Miss Morton." As they shook hands, he was struck by the sense of purpose in her face, so at variance with her youth.

When the door closed behind him she sat down again and stared round the room. She had always known that she and her grandmother were dependent on Philip Lameter's good nature for a home, but it had never been brought so forcibly to her notice before this moment. Her grandfather must have been a hard man to disinherit his wife and daughter for lack of a son. Lilac was glad that she had never known him.

The house seemed abnormally quiet. Yet, that was surely her imagination for Grandmother had hardly been a noisy person. Most of their evenings together were spent in sewing or reading with only an occasional remark passing between them. At the funeral neighbours had come to say all the right things. Then their support had been withdrawn, and Lilac was left mourning two losses with no tears left to cry.

The curtains were partly drawn, and the customary wreath hung on the front door. For three months she must wear black and avoid any places of gaiety. The room felt like it was closing in around her. The only sound was the ticking of the clock. She might sit here for hours, even days, until the darkness of her dress faded into the panelled walls and her bones crumbled.

She rose, shaking off the lethargy of grief. In her grandmother's room the bed had been stripped, the mattress cover smoothed tight. It was as if Barbara Lameter had never existed, never loved a man, been disappointed in bearing a daughter instead of a son, sorrowed for that daughter, and died at the end of it all. As if she had never been.

Lilac opened the wardrobe where her grandmother's clothes hung. She would ask Cook and Alice if there was anything they wanted and send the rest to the Ladies' Aid Society. The jewel case where Barbara kept her gems was on the dressing table. Lilac opened that too. Barbara's wedding ring had been buried with her; but there remained a set of garnet bracelets, a pearl necklace, two mourning rings in which were wound cuttings of her parents' and her daughter's hair, a pair of drop earrings with topazes in them, and a snuffbox with an ivory heart inlaid in the silver.

Lilac gazed at these items thoughtfully. They would fetch a good price, apart from the mourning rings. As she wondered how one went about selling jewellery, she noticed there were two layers of velvet. She lifted out the first layer and looked beneath. In the under compartment reposed a gold cross and chain, a child's tooth mounted in silver, a gold toothpick, with a further space beneath.

There Lilac found a small packet of letters, three in all, folded many times and tied with a length of black thread. She hesitated a moment then untied the string. Barbara was dead. There could be no harm in reading them now. They were all in the same delicate, slanting hand, the ink somewhat faded.

Morton Grange,
Keighley,
Yorkshire,
5 February, 1799.

Dearest Mama,

Your last letter brought me joy and pain. Joy, since it was from you, and pain since you tell me that I must endure the life I have chosen. But here it is like the end of the world—the people so harsh and savage. I shall be happy to sail for the New World where I am sure the natives will be more friendly. We have not yet heard when we are to go, which is a great irritant to Robert. He burns to start his work at once, but the bishop keeps finding a dozen excuses to delay matters. Meanwhile, I take your advice and endeavour to render myself useful to my parents-in-law. Though I fear they regard me as sadly frivolous. You would be astonished to learn that a lace collar is a sign of depravity. I go for walks on the moors. Though it is very bracing in this remote spot, it is a relief to get away from the house. I wish we were on more friendly terms with the neighbours, but the nearest is Mr Chance Harlan and he and Robert are at outs. Despite his youth Mr Harlan leads an existence that is extremely dissipated and refuses to be admonished for it.

I fear this letter is becoming a sad list of complaints so I will draw to a close, assuring you that I am in excellent health and place my confidence in the Lord who directs all our steps,

I am, dear Mama,
Your loving and obedient daughter,
Mary Lameter Morton.

The next was dated in June of the same year.

Dearest Mama,

It pleases me that my recent news gave you

pleasure. I am no longer feeling so sickly in the mornings, and I do rest every day. The weather is fine, and the lilac is out. I walk a little still and have tried to persuade Robert to accompany me as he spends too much time brooding over the recent rebuff he has received from the bishop. I tell him that if it is not the Lord's will that we sail to America then we are destined for some more important task, but he does not listen to me. Most of his time is devoted to rescue work in the Bradford Mission, and I see little of him. His parents also take little notice of me, beyond re-marking that females with blue eyes frequently die in childbirth, which is not, I think, a scientific fact.

I must end this as I am running out of space and do not wish to begin a new sheet,
Your loving and obedient daughter,
Mary Lameter Morton.

Lilac frowned, read the letter over again, and turned to the final one. It was dated in September of that year and was very brief.

Dearest Mama,
I do wish you would visit us. I don't know why but I am so terribly afraid. I tell myself there is no reason for it, but that doesn't help. Sometimes I think I must be going mad, save that I know that I am not. If you could talk to Robert, for he will not heed one word. Oh, do, do try to come,
Mary.

Four months later Lilac had been born.

"Your mama came home at Christmas just before your birth," Grandmother had said. "She was very sad and shocked by what had happened to your poor papa. Then when you were born the Lord took her."

Save that it now looks as if the Lord had not taken Papa

to America to be killed by the savages. Unless the bishop had changed his mind and sent Papa to the Mission-field after all. But that last letter had been written in September from Morton Grange, and in the three months that followed there surely hadn't been time to sail to America and get killed.

Lilac's eyes returned to the last letter. The words seemed to leap out at her, desperate in their pleading. "I don't know why but I am so terribly afraid."

=6=

It was as if she had known all along she was going up to Yorkshire, but of course, that wasn't so. Yet the finding of the letters had released questions which had been in her mind a long time but never uttered.

Why had her Morton grandparents never wanted to see her? She could not recall a single letter or message from them in her whole life. Their son had died a martyr, and yet they ignored the existence of their grandchild.

She suspected that to arrive in Keighley as Miss Lilac Mary Morton would ensure she never found out anything. Better to go there incognito, but Lilac had not the faintest idea how to set about it. She spent hours puzzling out the best course to take.

Her dilemna was solved in a most unexpected way. A few days after the funeral, as she sat drinking coffee in the morning room, Lieutenant Alfred Watson was announced. The sound of his rank brought her to her feet, her cheeks flushing with nervous excitement. Then the sound of his name sat her down again, cool once more, as a slice of cucumber.

"Good morning, Lieutenant Watson." She offered him a chair, wondering what he wanted to see her about. Perhaps Peter Wentworth had entrusted him with a message to deliver, but that was unlikely since Alfred was the brother of the bride.

"Hope I'm not disturbing you, Miss Lilac?" He sat stiffly on the chair.

"Not in the least. I am happy to have a visitor," she answered him. "After a funeral I find one misses company more than anything, but people don't call. Maybe they fear that death is catching."

Alfred started to laugh, then evidently remembered that he was in a house of mourning and looked embarrassed instead.

"Wonderful, the way you're bearing up," he murmured.

"My grandmother was a very practical woman," Lilac said. "She would not have expected the world to come to an end because she wasn't in it any longer. May I offer you some coffee?"

"Thank you, no. Just finished breakfast. As a matter of fact, the truth is, I escaped."

"I beg your pardon?" Lilac was startled.

"From talk of weddings," he said gloomily. "Weddings are for the ladies. I can't whip up much interest in whether Amelia has satin or silk flowers on her skirt."

"So you fled here?" Lilac was amused.

"For a few minutes, if you don't object. The club ain't open yet, even if I was welcome there."

"Whatever did you do in the club?" she enquired with interest.

"More a case of what I didn't do," he admitted. "Didn't pay. End of the month. Papa being difficult. Wedding coming up. So I have to amuse myself in other ways. Not that I wouldn't have come to see you anyway, Miss Lilac. Old friends and all that."

"It's very kind of you, Alfred." She smiled.

"The truth is," he said fumblingly. "I've been thinking. You all by yourself. Me off to India in a couple of weeks. My commanding officer keen on the idea . . . thought I'd enquire."

"Enquire about what?"

"Well . . . weddings. And the two of us being such old friends, and Papa telling me I ought to settle, and I am rather fond of you when all's said and done."

Lilac stared at Alfred's good-natured face, now gone slightly pink. "Are you proposing marriage to me?" she asked at last.

"Seems the decent thing to do," he said earnestly. "You by yourself, and my commanding officer telling us that marriage settles a man down and all that."

"It's terribly kind of you," Lilac answered, not sure whether to laugh or burst into tears.

"Glad to oblige," Alfred said.

"But it really wouldn't do. We are not in the least in love, you know. We are excellent as friends, but as a married couple we would not suit at all."

"You really don't think so?"

"I am quite certain," she said firmly. "Though I do appreciate your asking."

"Feeling a mite worried about you, to speak truth," he said, flushing even deeper. "No protector until your uncle returns."

"Perhaps there is a way in which you can help me," Lilac said, regarding him thoughtfully.

"Anything I can do. Be awfully pleased," he assured her promptly.

"I intend to go up to Yorkshire," she told him. "My father's people came from there, and I have a fancy to visit. However, it would be difficult for me if I went up in my own name . . . an old family feud. You understand."

"Lord, yes. Family set-tos are the absolute limit," he agreed. "Better for you to stay out of it altogether, you know. And Yorkshire is a very wet county, they tell me."

"I wish to rent a house near Keighley," Lilac pressed on, unheeding. "I would take it for six months in the name of Lily Watson. The difficulty is that I don't know how to go about it."

"Better not go about it at all," he advised. "Might be complications. Risky business, this changing names."

"Then I'll be Lily. I suppose I could keep my own surname. It is not so uncommon. I am determined to do this, Alfred, but I would like to undertake it with your help."

"You want me to rent a house for you? There are agents for that sort of thing, or I could ask around discreetly."

"Oh, it must be very discreet," she warned him. "I do not wish anyone else to know what I am about. If you could make the necessary arrangements—I realise there is little time."

"Might cost a bit. Short notice and all that," he said doubtfully.

"I would not wish you to go above three hundred pounds."

"Oh, for that I believe something might be contrived," Alfred said, "but I still think—"

"Pray don't," Lilac said hastily. "I rely on you absolutely as one of my dearest friends. You might be the means whereby an ancient feud is brought to an end."

"I will do my best."

His tone was solemn as any knight's setting off to reclaim the Holy Land from the Saracens. Alfred, she thought, had a romantic soul.

"There is one other matter." She sat up straight and endeavoured to look businesslike. "I have some jewellery, very old-fashioned and not suitable for me at all. I don't suppose you would know where it might be possible to sell or pawn it, do you?"

"Pawn is better," he said promptly. "Raises less cash, but you can get the stuff back at the end."

"Pawn them then; and Alfred, as you are acting as my agent in this matter, I insist upon your taking ten percent."

"Good Lord, no," he protested. "Wouldn't hear of it."

"You could pay back some of your debts before you left for India without having to apply to your papa," she suggested.

"Must agree that idea's appealing," he muttered. "I would call it a loan though and repay bit by bit. Absolutely insist on that."

"Very well. A loan if you like."

He was quite scarlet now. "I can give you a note of hand."

"Nonsense, Alfred. I trust you as a man of honour," she said briskly. "I shall give you the jewels with a note of authorization in case the pawnbroker wishes to know how you came by them."

"Usually they don't enquire too closely," Alfred said, revealing his familiarity with the habits of pawnbrokers.

"All this must be a close secret between us," she warned, rising. "I do trust your discretion with confidence, dear Alfred."

"My lips are sealed," said Alfred gallantly.

He really was rather a dear. She gave him the jewellery and watched him go down the front steps. He didn't really want to marry her at all, but he had thought it polite to make the offer. Perhaps nobody would ever want to marry her. The prospect was depressing.

Meanwhile, she had not expected to see Alfred again for at least a week; but he was back two days later, looking decidedly more cheerful.

"Raised two thousand guineas on the jewellery," he said triumphantly.

"Alfred, that's wonderful. However did you contrive?"

"Decent man," he said vaguely. "He . . . er . . . knows me by sight. You are sure about the ten percent?"

"Will that cover your debts?"

"Well, not exactly," he admitted, "but it will keep them quiet."

"Take twenty-five percent then," she said recklessly. "No, I insist. I shall have fifteen hundred guineas, and I cannot see how I could possibly spend that much in Yorkshire."

"I will certainly pay you back," he said gratefully. "I don't suppose you'd thought of putting the money on a horse? There's the sweetest little filly—"

"No horses, Alfred. Not for any of the money."

"Just a thought. Probably you're right." He looked faintly regretful.

"Certainly I am right. Now about my renting a house."

"Wonderful news there," he said, beaming. "Happened to be talking to a friend of mine. Fellow officer, very discreet, so there's no worry on that score. His parents died last year. Typhus, a nasty business. Left him a house in Yorkshire."

"Where in Yorkshire?"

"Place called Oxenhope. Not far from Keighley. Decent place. Use of carriage and horses. He tells me there is a skeleton staff."

"That sounds absolutely splendid," she said with enthusiasm.

"Three hundred for the six months. Told him it was for a particular friend of mine."

"I will see that you have the rent for him by the end of the week. You have been a tremendous help, Alfred."

"Only hope I'm doing the right thing by helping out," he said. "You're sure you wouldn't rather get married? I'm willing to go ahead, you know."

"Quite sure, Alfred. In what name am I renting this?"

Lily Morton. Thought of saying Watson; but I'd mentioned you were a friend, not a relative."

"And it is a solemn secret between us?"

"A sacred trust," he assured her. "But what are you going to tell everybody else? If you vanish it'll cause worry. Mama's uncommonly fond of you."

"I am going up to stay with my father's people," Lilac said promptly. "I shall leave word for my uncle to that effect. I am taking Alice with me. I shall be obliged to tell her a little, but she is devoted to me and will certainly agree."

It was all going much more smoothly than Lilac had dared to hope. At least making all the preparations ensured that her mind was occupied. She would leave off mourning when she reached Yorkshire since, if she were still in black, her movements would be restricted by custom. She hoped that Grandmother, wherever she was now, would not disapprove too highly.

Lilac debated with herself whether or not to confide in Mr Green but decided against it. He would certainly try to put obstacles in the way of her going. He would regard the trip as a vastly unsuitable one. Therefore, it was best to keep her own counsel.

There was, of course, no difficulty with the Watsons who were busy with the wedding preparations and had no time to spare for anything else. Amelia called a few days after the house in Yorkshire had been rented, but she could talk of nothing but the presents that were flooding in.

"So many that we will require another ship to carry them all. I meant to come and see you before this, but I have been so occupied with the unwrapping of gifts."

"Which reminds me that I have one for you," Lilac began, only to be interrupted by a squeal.

"Heavens, Lilac, I wasn't hinting. Oh, but I shall be mortified if you take it that I was hinting."

"No, of course you were not," Lilac said. "I really do have a gift, though not a very original one, I fear."

The present had come from a stock of trays and coffee-pots which Grandmother drew upon whenever any of her acquaintances was married. As such, it was in perfect taste but completely impersonal. Still, Amelia greeted the gift with cries of delight.

"It is quite á la mode, Lilac! Peter and I will so enjoy drinking our morning coffee from it."

The innocent words conjured up a picture of intimacy that gave Lilac a pang. "I believe that in India they drink more tea," she said lightly, all the same.

"It is difficult to imagine that soon I shall be in foreign lands," Amelia said solemnly. "I am occasionally a trifle nervous thinking of it, but Peter says I will soon settle down."

She had mentioned his name several times, taking a natural delight in bringing it into the conversation. Lilac no longer winced. Instead, she refused to allow herself to think about it and, consequently, was able to answer quite placidly.

"Oh, I am sure he is right. Caroline Fitzroy is already in Calcutta, is she not? I think she was always a most amusing girl."

"They will none of them be as amusing as you," Amelia said, briefly mournful. "I sometimes wonder what in the world I am doing to be sailing off to the far corner of the world and leaving my very best friend behind."

"I may not be long in London," Lilac took the opportunity to remark. "My papa's family came from Yorkshire, and I look forward to paying them a visit. I would take Alice with me."

"How strange it will be," Amelia mused, "when you and I are so far separate. I know I will never make another friend I love so well."

Her words were an ending, Lilac thought, as if she had closed one book and was now prepared to open another full of different characters.

Alice's reaction to the proposed trip was eminently satisfactory.

"Are you going to find out the truth behind a mystery?" she enquired.

"Something like that," Lilac said cautiously. "I cannot understand why my paternal grandparents never asked after me or had any desire to see me. I am taking another name. So please recall I am now Miss Lily."

"Won't they recognise Morton?" Alice asked.

"I thought of that," Lilac confessed, "but it is not an uncommon name. So I will risk it. There's a possibility I will not even meet them, but in that case we will have lost nothing."

"It's going to be an adventure, ain't it?" Alice said happily.

That was how she must consider it, Lilac decided. She was embarking on an adventure, and that was much more sensible than sitting here grieving because Lieutenant Peter Wentworth was marrying Amelia.

I too, thought Lilac, *am opening a book full of new characters.*

=7=

THE STAGE WENT only as far as Keighley after which they would need to hire transport to the house Lilac had rented. Sladen Hall was the address. She assumed its location would be known, but Alfred on his last visit had been somewhat vague.

"All moors and mills round there," he said. "Not many decent places, if you ask me—not that I ever visited."

He had come to assure her that he would speedily repay the five hundred guineas. Lilac thought he'd probably do that as long as a nice little filly wasn't running in the meantime.

"Write to me now," he cautioned. "Care of the regiment. Don't want you getting into any difficulties."

She had promised though, even if she did come to grief, she failed to see how Alfred in India would be able to do much about it. She left a note for her uncle with Mr Briggs. However, it was more than likely she'd be home again before Philip Lameter arrived.

The first leg of the journey took them up to Nottingham where they stayed overnight in a coaching inn. Lilac, who had never been so far from London, felt her spirits lift as they rolled farther north. She was still sore at heart at the prospect of the wedding that would take place in two days time, but at least she would not have to witness it. Instead, she might have the pleasure of being greeted by long-lost relatives. Lilac reminded herself that those same relatives had considered a lace collar the height of depravity, and sent Alice to order supper.

Several of the passengers had left the coach when they boarded it again the next morning, and others had taken their places. None of them looked very interesting, and Lilac was glad of the English reserve which kept conversation to a minimum. Her sex and her mourning weeds prevented her fellow travellers from engaging her in talk. Alice, who mistrusted anyone not born within the sound of Bow Bells, sat like a fierce, young dragon at her side, meeting the most tentative smiles with a cold and hostile stare.

Meanwhile, the roads became steeper, the horses straining. There were fewer trees. They passed several blackened structures which Lilac guessed correctly to be mills. She had heard that children worked in them. At least she was not in a position where it was necessary to seek employment. She had worried a little about the story she might be required to provide since she was somewhat young to be setting up housekeeping alone and had hit upon the notion of invalidism.

Sickly, young ladies were often sent into more bracing climates and were not expected to take too strenuous a part in local gaieties.

It was late afternoon when the stage rolled into Keighley to the accompaniment of loud cheers from the more vociferous of the passengers. A journey accomplished without breakdown, robbery, or the fatality of some elderly passenger was clearly a triumph. Alice, however, shot Lilac a darkling look as they climbed down into the cobbled yard of the stagepost.

"That thing," she said, jerking her bonneted head towards the vehicle, "has shaken loose all me teeth."

"Nonsense, Alice. It was a most comfortable ride," Lilac chided. "Now we must hire a carriage and get our luggage transferred."

That proved easier said than done. At first nobody

seemed to have heard of Sladen Hall, and Lilac had begun to experience a touch of panic when a man, shifting his bulk from the wall against which he had been leaning, volunteered the information that Sladen Hall was "ower t'moor and near t'beck."

"Can we procure a carriage to take us there?" she asked.

"Reckon."

"Presumably that means we can. Could you see to it for me?"

By way of reply he gave her a long, slow look and shambled off.

"The stage," said Alice with meaning, "turns back to London first thing in the morning."

"Hush. I believe transport is coming."

A somewhat delapidated carriage was being hitched to an equally shabby horse in a far corner of the yard. The man to whom Lilac had spoken jerked his thumb in that direction.

"Seth'll drive. Be three shillings," he said.

Seth looked younger than both carriage and horses, and was as taciturn as his friend. He shifted the luggage with a couple of grunts and made no effort to help the ladies over the high step.

"How far is it?" Lilac paused to address him.

"An hour driving, three walking," he informed her.

"Thank you." She stepped up into the musty interior as Alice muttered that they would both likely be murdered.

The bustle of the town fell away behind them as they turned onto a steep, unpaved road. Seth appeared to be a competent driver. Lilac comforted herself with that thought and hung on to the strap as the vehicle jolted over the rough surface. Through the grimy windows she could see at each side a featureless expanse of grass that rose and dipped to meet a sky dyed scarlet by the dying sun.

This truly did look a little like the end of the world, Lilac reflected. She felt a keen sympathy for the mother she had never known who came here to meet her new relatives before going to the New World: save that it looked as if she had never made the voyage at all.

Alice whimpered faintly as they lurched over a tussock, closing her eyes. The sound stirred Lilac out of her despondent thoughts.

"There will be a much better conveyance at Sladen Hall," said Lilac by way of encouragement. "Only think, Alice, this will be a splendid adventure to tell our grandchildren."

"If we live to 'ave any," was her maid's gloomy reply.

It is doubtful that I will ever marry now, Lilac thought. I don't believe I will fall in love again, and I would never take a husband for any other reason. I will probably do good works instead.

The prospect of that made her feel as gloomy as Alice looked, and Lilac hastily turned her attention to the landscape again. A purple haze was stealing over the grass, and above the clopping of the hooves she could hear the keening of the wind. Here and there pinpoints of light sprang up, the proof of civilization, she told herself, and tried to take her mind off present discomfort by cogitating as to who her neighbours might be. As she wished to meet the Mortons, it would be wise to go about a little in local society. That is—if there was some local society. Up to now she had seen no evidence of it.

The darkness was closing in rapidly, taking the purple haze with it, turning the grass to sable. She repressed a shiver and fixed her mind on the hot supper she would order when they arrived. Alfred had assured her that a message announcing the arrival of the new tenant had been despatched.

Then a pistol shot rang out so suddenly and loudly that both she and Alice cried out. A figure was galloping towards them over the rise.

"Oh, lawks," Alice moaned. "It's a highwayman."

Lilac felt her heart shudder. She had sewn the money Alfred had obtained for the jewels into the hem of her petticoat and into the lining of her muff, leaving only a couple of hundred guineas in her purse. She hoped the robber would not insist on a personal search. Meanwhile, the carriage was slowing and stopping. Obviously, Seth and his friend were part of the gang. She had been a fool to trust herself to strangers.

"Beck's flooded," a male voice called above the wind. "You'll not get through."

"Going t' Sladen Hall," Seth yelled back.

"The devil you are. What's your errand at Sladen?" The voice sounded surprised.

"Two wenches," Seth answered.

"Wenches at Sladen? Well, the world's looking brighter." The rider trotted nearer, leaning to the window. It was too dark to see his face, but Lilac gained an impression of harshness in a jutting nose and high cheekbones.

"Well, well," the man said and wheeled away again, calling over his shoulder, "Take the lower road. You can cut down past the forks."

The galloping of hooves mingled with the grinding of the carriage wheels over gravel as the carriage described a wide arc and entered what appeared to be a quarry path. At each side rocks reared black heads against a swirling sky.

"You see, Alice," Lilac said, "it was not a highwayman at all. Merely a neighbour wishing to save us discomfort."

"Trying to put us off our guard," Alice cried.

"Nonsense. We shall be there at any time now."

"Can't be too soon for me," Alice said fervently.

They were climbing again. Lilac had a fleeting glimpse of a group of trees bent sideways by the wind, and then they plunged into darkness.

There were high walls at each side and ahead, as the carriage stopped, a pile of masonry that resolved itself into a building as grim and gaunt as a medieval castle. Not a light gleamed from any of the deep-mullioned windows, but Seth raised his voice, shouting, "Fanny. Fanny, there's folks come."

Somewhere a door opened and a woman, holding a lantern, appeared, the ends of the shawl about her head fluttering in the wind as she lifted the lantern and answered, "What folks? What are thee blathering on about, Seth Armstrong?"

"Two wenches," Seth said. "Come on't stage."

"I am the new tenant," Lilac said clearly, wrenching open the carriage door and clambering down into the yard. "Miss Lily Morton. A letter was sent. Did you not receive it?"

"Aye, we got a letter." The girl, who was not much older than Lilac, nodded.

"Saying that Miss Lily Morton had rented this house from Mr Sladen, Lieutenant Sladen of the —"

"Don't rightly know what it said," the girl interrupted. "Can't read good."

"Oh dear." Lilac turned to Alice who had climbed down at her side. "It looks as if we were not expected."

"I heard," Alice said grimly.

"Perhaps we had better go indoors," Lilac said. "The muddle can be sorted out. Alice, pay the fare and have the . . . have Seth bring in the luggage. Fanny, is it? Shall we go indoors?"

"Reckon," said Fanny and plunged into a doorway that led as far as Lilac could discern in the flare of the lantern light into a side passage.

Beyond the passage another door opened into a square antechamber, with a low fire burning on the hearth, and the remains of a meal on the table. Against the tea caddy on the high mantel shelf her letter of introduction was propped.

"Where are the other servants?" Lilac asked.

"Elijah's in't barn," Fanny said. "Tha wants him?"

"No, no. Leave him in't—I mean in the barn. Where is everybody else?"

"Just Elijah and me," Fanny said, unwinding her shawl and hanging the lantern on a hook. "Just us."

"I suppose thar's what 'e meant by a skeleton staff," Alice said.

"Only two of you to manage this entire place?" Lilac looked round.

"Nobody ever comes," Fanny said simply. Unwrapped from the voluminous shawl she was revealed as a rather pretty girl, her hair a tangled mass of gingery curls.

"Alice, what are we to do?" Lilac turned imploringly to the other.

Alice had taken a deep breath. Highwaymen were one thing, but here was a situation she could deal with since it involved practical action.

"You leave it all to me, Miss Li. . . Lily," she said confidently. "Looks like the place hasn't been kept up proper. Now, Fanny, is it? The mistress 'as come a long ways and she's fit to drop. We need clean linen on the beds and a couple of warming pans and a bite to eat. You'd best stir up Elijah to lend an 'and, and meanwhile the mistress ain't accustomed to sitting in kitchens. We'll need a fire in the main part of the house."

Lilac held her breath, afraid the slatternly girl would take exception to Alice's hectoring tone, but it seemed to have the desired effect.

"Pink room's clean," Fanny said. "Sleep there mysef at times."

"Tonight you'll find somewhere else," Alice informed her. "Right then, miss. We'll take a look at this 'ere pink room and get a fire going and be snug as bugs in two ticks."

She turned to give Seth, who had just entered with the luggage, the fare and turned back, saying briskly, "Now let's be on our way."

The way was a rambling one along winding stone corridors and up twisting stairs until Fanny opened a door and led them into a large and unexpectedly charming apartment hung with faded pink silk and no more than a spattering of dust over the carved furniture.

"This looks more like it." There was satisfaction in Alice's tone. "The fire's laid ready too. We must just pray that the chimney don't smoke. Now, miss, you make yourself comfy, and I'll soon 'ave this place looking like 'ome."

Alice was herself again, bustling about and sending Fanny, who seemed to have bowed to a stronger personality, skittering to fetch Elijah. Lilac sat down in the large chair by the window and closed her eyes. She felt bone weary and not a little inclined to regret having come here in the first place. It was typical of Alfred to have been rooked, she thought crossly, all her earlier gratitude evaporating. He hadn't troubled to make detailed enquiries at all. The house had evidently stood empty for years, and Lieutenant Sladen had inherited a white elephant.

She must have dozed a spell because the next thing she heard was Alice's voice.

"The linen's clean and dry, so that's a mercy. It's plain there ain't been a mistress round this place for years. I've 'ad a word with Fanny, who tells me that Mr and Mrs Sladen 'ad the 'ouse willed to 'em by a cousin, and never came near it. Can't say as I blame 'en for it'd cost a fortune to keep up proper. Fanny and Elijah are brother and sister, get paid by messenger once a year. The other servants got bored and left. No visitors and nowhere to go except them dratted moors. I've got a nice drop of soup and a broiled trout which will settle your insides after the jolting they 'ad. I tell you straight, miss, mine won't ever be the same again."

In the course of her monologue she had got Lilac out of her travelling clothes and into her nightgown. The clean linen was being laid on the bed, and Fanny came in with a warming pan.

"I explained as how you're a bit of an invalid, miss," Alice said, plumping up pillows, "and need to 'ave everything right and dandy. Her and me'll get on a treat, just you see. Now, if you will 'op in I'll bring the tray."

"Where will you sleep?" Lilac asked as she obeyed.

"There's a room next to this that'll suit me for the moment," Alice said cheerfully. "Tomorrow I shall go through this place until it's like a new pin."

"It'll take you more than a day," Lilac said.

"We've got six months, 'aven't we?" Alice retorted. "It'll give me something to do, for walk out on them perishing moors I will not."

The soup was hot and the trout was fresh. Obviously there was no shortage of food in these remote parts. Fanny had lit the fire, and the crackling of the burning wood made a pleasant sound. By the morning light it would be possible to see how much work needed to be done.

"I'll leave the lantern, miss," Alice said, taking the tray. "There are plenty more downstairs. If you need anything just ring. The bells are working which is a surprise and a blessing. Now, Fanny, you and me will take a bite of supper and leave the mistress in peace."

The door closed and the only sound besides the crackling of the fire was the noise of the wind gusting down the chimney. Lilac had expected to weep a little for her lost love, but the last thought in her mind before she fell asleep was that they had forgotten to enquire the name of the man who had warned them away from the flooded beck.

=8=

IN THE MORNING Lilac woke up to the singing of a bird outside her window and the decidedly unmusical sound of Alice singing as well. Sunlight was flooding the room, revealing the dust and the faded draperies more cruelly than lamplight had done. Yet the apartment was still charming. The door opened, and Alice came in, mobcap on head, tray in her hands. She looked as if she had been in service here for years, though her first words were a complaint.

"Never in my entire life did I ever see such a state as everything's in. Rack and ruin, miss. Sheer rack and ruin, I tell you. Makes you wonder what the world's coming to. It will take the 'ole six months and then some to get this place to rights."

"The breakfast looks good," Lilac interrupted. "I can perfectly well get up for it though."

"Not with the dining room in the state it is," Alice said firmly. "Anyway it looks more natural for an invalid to 'ave breakfast in bed. Now, eat up and I'll get on with the unpacking."

"What have you found out?" Lilac began to attack the breakfast.

"Not much," Alice said. "Mr Sladen who lived here twenty years back got 'imself killed fighting the Frenchies and the place went to his cousins, but they never came up to see it."

"Lieutenant Sladen's parents. They died. So the servants stayed on?"

Fanny and Elijah were born here," Alice said, holding up a petticoat and shaking the creases out of it. "Their parents were the cook and butler, but they died ten years back. So them two stayed on. The others left. Oh, and the man who added ten years to me life last night is called Chance Harland."

". . . Mr Chance Harland and Robert are at outs. Mr Harland leads a life that is extremely dissipated and refuses to be admonished for it . . ." Mary Morton had written that in the second brief letter she had sent to her mother from Morton Grange. If there was anything for her to learn it might be he who would know.

"I hope that the carriage and horses are in a better condition than the house," Lilac said aloud.

"I've been that shocked at the 'ouse that I've not dared stick me nose in the barn," Alice said.

"I won't want the carriage anyway," Lilac said. "I think I'll go for a ride later on, but first I'll go round the house and we can work out what to do."

It was not as vast as she had imagined the previous night when darkness had magnified it it was still a good size, with long corridors and staircases that twisted about themselves and tiny rooms tucked away between the larger chambers. Everywhere was the evidence of neglect. The main structure seemed sound but the cornices were mouldering. The curtains had provided banquets for moths, and the floors hadn't seen polish in a decade.

"It was a lovely house once," she said, "but it's been neglected."

"You can say that in capital letters, miss," Alice agreed. "Well, I'm a lady's maid but not too proud to turn me 'and to a bit of cleaning. To tell you the truth I'm itching to start."

"I'd better meet Elijah," Lilac said.

"Waiting in the kitchen," Alice said. "I knew you'd want to see 'im. He's ten years older than Fanny and not as bright, so I suppose that's why they stayed on."

Elijah was large, amiable, and reminded her irresistibly of Alfred.

"This place is in a dreadful state," she began severely, only to be floored by his "Aye, that it is."

"Well, now that Alice is here it must be set to rights."

"Aye, that it must," Elijah agreed.

"What of the carriage and horses? I was informed they were for use."

"Bottom of t'coach fell out years back," Fanny interposed.

"Aye," said Elijah. "That it did."

"And the horse? Can the horse still walk?"

"We've two horses, Miss," Fanny said. "One's old, but t'other's now but a foal."

"In that case I believe that I will take a walk," Lilac said.

"You might get lost," Alice said, looking anxious.

"I don't intend to go far. There are grounds here, so I will keep within the boundaries of the park. It's such a beautiful day."

It was indeed one of those days that come sometimes at the latter end of summer to make one forget that autumn lurks around the corner. Sladen Hall was, she saw, built in a hollow, its grey walls crenellated, its courtyard overshadowed by ivy that clung thickly to the stone and gave an antique aspect to the whole. Beyond the walled path the moor stretched to the horizon, but a bridle path leading past the stables led into grounds that had clearly remained unweeded for twenty years. Lilac took the bridle path and was soon pushing her way through tangled briar and past bushes that spread their branches for the unwary. She congratulated herself on having donned a serviceable dress and a pair of thick shoes since her thinner clothes would have been quickly ripped. There were wild strawberries growing and a variety of fruit and nut trees.

She pushed aside a long tendril of creeper and was overwhelmed by the scent of lilac. There were lilac bushes here, growing so thickly that it was almost impossible to find space between them. The perfume was intoxicating. She stood still, letting her senses be lulled into a kind of dreaming. This was a place for lovers. She could almost believe that when she opened her eyes again a lover would be standing there, formed out of the substance of her longing; but there were only her and the lilacs.

She turned, taking a narrower path that twisted into the high bracken and found herself on the moor again with the heather-clad turf sloping down to an expanse of rippling water. That must be the beck, flooded beyond its banks, the arch of a bridge glinting grey-gold in the sun. This was no formal London park where children sailed boats on the pond while nursemaids gossipped. This was untamed land, its beauty subtle and haunting. She began to run for the sheer joy of running, her hair whipping free from the scarf with which she had bound it, her feet trampling heather. At the top of the rise she sank down onto the grass, lifting her face to the breeze.

"You'll be the wench come to Sladen Hall," a voice observed.

Lilac sat bolt upright, her eyes widening, her mouth opening. He was on foot this morning, a riding crop in his hand. His hair was not black as she had thought but dark red, like the pelt of a fox; and his eyes were bronze. That was the only shade she could think of to describe them as she sat staring, her mouth still open.

"That means we're to have tenants at Sladen, I suppose," he remarked. "Well, it's time someone came to restore life to the old place. When do they arrive?"

"They're already here," Lilac said faintly.

"The owners or tenants?"

"Tenants."

"Then shouldn't you be making ready for their comfort instead of cavorting about here?"

He thought her a domestic. Lilac opened her mouth to correct him and said instead in as accurate an imitation of

Alice as she could muster, "I've got 'alf an hour off, sir. The mistress said as it was all right."

"Who is your mistress?"

"Miss Morton, sir."

"Morton."

The exclamation broke from him with such force that she was startled. She was more startled an instant later when he suddenly leaned and hauled her to her feet, seizing her chin and forcing her face to the light.

"You're Miss Morton," he said flatly. "You can't be Mary. We heard she died."

"What makes you think—?" She jerked free and took a step backwards.

"Only Mary Morton had eyes like those," he said. "You must be—"

"Lilac Mary Morton," she said, resignedly, "but I am here incognito."

"Using the same surname?"

"I hoped it might be a common one in these parts," she explained, "but it seems I am already found out."

"Only by the eyes. I never forgot those eyes. I am—"

"Mr Chance Harland. Yes, I know."

"Then you have the advantage of me. You are Lilac, you say?"

"Mary Morton was my mother," she said.

"Your mother!" again the sharp exclamation. The bronze eyes had darkened.

"Did you know her, sir?"

"Did I . . . ? Yes, I was acquainted with her." He spoke wryly as if to hide some deeper emotion.

"She died when I was born," Lilac said. "I was brought up in London by my maternal grandmother, but she also died recently."

"Mary Morton's daughter." He shook his head slowly, whistling softly through his teeth.

"Here incognito," she reminded him.

"As you said. Why the devil came you to these parts at all?"

"To meet my other grandparents," Lilac said, too surprised to resent his method of questioning. "I have never heard from them, you see; and I have wondered why. So I decided to come and find out. There may have been a family quarrel or something."

"The Mortons are dead," he told her. "It would have been a miracle if you had ever heard from them. They died years ago."

"But not before I was born, surely?"

"About ten years back," he said curtly. "They disapproved of your mother, considered her to be frivolous. I suppose that is why they never communicated. Anyway, they are both dead now."

She had never thought of that possibility, and a pang of disappointment went through her.

"And Morton Grange is unoccupied?" she enquired.

"I have no idea." His voice was still cold. "I have better things to do than fret about my neighbours."

"That is why you were so uninterested in the possibility of Sladen Hall being occupied, I suppose?" she said sweetly.

"My own property is not too far distant. Miss Morton, if you have come to Yorkshire in order to discover some unknown facts about your late mother's life, I fear you are wasting your time. The sensible course of action would have been to write and make enquiry. Thus you would have saved yourself the trouble and expense of a long journey for nothing."

"But you knew my mother."

"Only slightly. I met her once or twice. At that time I was a rather impressionable youth of seventeen, and the colour of her eyes was sufficiently unusual to attract my notice. However, as I say, my acquaintanceship with her was of the slightest."

He gave a brief bow that was more like a nod and turned

away, striding back over the crest of the hill without a further glance. Lilac stared after him, irritation mingling with her disappointment. Chance Harland had no breeding, she decided. Not one word of sympathy for her wasted journey, only a brusque rebuttal of her attempts to find out anything. In a handsome man such ill manners would have been distasteful, but in a harsh-featured individual with hair like the pelt of a fox they were inexcusable.

The bright morning was spoilt. Lilac was suddenly in a foot-stamping mood. She reminded herself, however, that she was seventeen and an independent and mature lady and walked back to the great house where Alice was up to her eyes and deep in her element, scurrying between kitchen and drawing room, chivving Fanny and Elijah who seemed not to mind being ordered about by a complete stranger.

"We're starting on the pink room," she announced. "It'll be ready for you by the time you go to bed. After that we'll do one room a day. 'Ope that suits?"

"I'll leave it to you, Alice." Her tone must have sounded dispirited because the other peered at her, remarking, "You don't sound as if you 'ad a nice walk."

"I met our neighbour, Mr Harland. He is most uncouth."

"I could 'ave told you that last night," Alice said. "Frightening the daylights out of us like that."

"Well, he did save us from driving into the beck," Lilac said, suddenly contrary.

"When all's said and done, a beck's only a bit of a stream." Alice said. "It ain't a raging torrent."

"I found a garden," Lilac remembered. "A lovely garden, hidden away in the midst of all the weeds. Nothing in it but lilacs."

"Bit late in the season, ain't it?"

"They are in their last blooming, I suppose. It would be nice to clear the garden too."

"Be winter before we get round to that," Alice said, pessimistically. "The winters 'ere sound perishing, miss. Places cut off by the snow and nothing to do."

"We must lay in supplies then, for I am determined to remain," Lilac said, an obstinate set to her pretty mouth. "Mr Harland guessed who I was by the by. I have my mother's eyes, it seems."

"Then he'd be able to tell you—" Alice began.

"Nothing. Not that I really deigned to ask. My father's people died some time since, and they disapproved of my mother which is evidently why they never communicated with me. It is very provoking."

"Does that mean we can go 'ome?" Alice asked eagerly.

Lilac hesitated. The temptation to run back to the comfortable and well-run home where she had spent all her life was strong, but if she went back so soon she would have to endure visits from Mrs Watson who would descend upon her with the kindest intentions to give her the minutest details of the wedding. Worse, Amelia herself was still there, awaiting passage to India, and Amelia engaged had been bad enough. Amelia married would be intolerable.

"We'll stay on for a while," she said at last. "If I can procure a good riding horse I may go over to Oxenhope to look at the house where my parents lived just after their marriage. I don't suppose Fanny or Elijah made any comments on the name of Morton?"

"I could ask," Alice said doubtfully, "but I don't 'old with gossiping with the staff."

"You are quite right. We'll say nothing."

"And there don't appear to be nothing to find out anyway," Alice said.

Lilac was not so sure about that. There had been a suppressed violence in Chance Harland's reaction to his discovery of her identity. She had the feeling he could have said more.

Leaving the maid to bustle the neglected household into some semblance of order, Lilac went back to the main part of the house. The front door opened into a large, square hall with twin staircases mounting to the upper storeys and chambers leading off from it: a drawing room that had not been touched for years, the drapes pitted with moth holes; a dining room with a row of portraits so thick with dust that it was no longer possible to discern the lineaments of the features of those portrayed; a long, narrow chamber with a spinet, the keys yellowed to deep ivory. Yet, when Lilac touched them they responded with an unexpectedly sweet sound like the ghost of a tune. It was a thousand pities that she could not play, she thought.

There were several smaller chambers leading out of one another and, at the back, a tiny room, which she mistook at first for a broom cupboard. Instead of brushes and mops, however, it held piles of books and ledgers which Lilac guessed to be the estate accounts. She picked up one of the heavy volumes, blowing on the cover to rid it of the dust, and suppressed a sneeze as a cloud flew up into her face. It was not, as she had thought, an account book but an exercise book. On the inner page was printed in curling script:

This book belongs to Chance Harland,
of Sladen Hall
in the county of Yorkshire,
in the Year of our Lord, 1790

=9=

LILAC STARED AT the inscription for a long moment. He had mentioned nothing of the fact that Sladen Hall had been his home. He had referred to it as the "old place," but she had assumed that he spoke as a neighbour. She turned the pages with a growing curiosity, seeing that it was a series of simple arithmetical problems, suitable for a child of about seven. He would have been an unattractive child, she thought, with a mop of reddish hair and those odd, bronze-coloured eyes. He had been a sharp little boy too. Most of the calculations were correct. It would be interesting to find out if there were other exercise books in the pile and if they contained some clue as to why he had lived here.

Meanwhile, she must obtain a horse.

Elijah, when applied to for advice scratched his head and opined that the horse already in residence might serve if she wasn't planning on racing him. Lilac assured him that she would be content if the animal went at a gentle trot and instructed him to find and clean a lady's saddle for her. She was determined to take a look, if only from the outside, at the place where her mother had spent less than a year of married life.

For the rest of the day she occupied herself in making sketches and drawing up lists of how she expected the house to look when the cleaning was finished. Houses, like people, ought not to be neglected. Already her bedroom was vastly improved with the faded drapes hanging damply in the breeze that came through the open casement and the floor beeswaxed until it shone.

The horse, which went by the wildly inappropriate name of Pegasus, was soul mate to Diamond. Nevertheless, he would have to suffice until she could find something better, and the animal had been well cared for. The saddle was old and the leather slightly cracked, but that also would have to serve. Accordingly, the next morning, ignoring Alice's protestations that she was sure to get lost, Lilac mounted up.

"Now if you will point me in the direction of Oxenhope?" She smiled down at Fanny who had come out into the stable yard.

"T'other road from Keighley," Fanny said, "South."

"Thank you. I shall be back this afternoon." Lilac urged Pegasus into what he considered a lively trot but was actually more in the nature of a gentle stroll.

The moor dipped down to the road which, to Lilac's relief, was clearly signposted. She had taken the precaution of bringing with her a flask of water since neither Fanny nor Elijah seemed certain of the exact distance. She soon found that on such a bright morning the leisurely pace at which she had perforce to travel was soothing rather than not. There was an occasional cottage along the way. She would have liked to stop and make the acquaintance of whoever lived in them, but the shyness engendered by city dwelling proved a barrier. This was, in any case, the first time in her life that she had ridden unaccompanied, and she revelled in the unfamiliar sense of freedom.

Oxenhope was a smaller town that Keighley had appeared to be from her brief glimpse of it. There was a large market square with a respectable inn. She left Pegasus in the charge of an ostler and went into the small dining chamber at the back to order luncheon.

In Yorkshire the fair sex evidently had more independence than was often the case elsewhere, since nobody looked askance at a young lady without escort. Lilac enjoyed her meal and, paying for it, enquired the whereabouts of Morton Grange. To her surprise the waiter hesitated before he answered.

"Tha's sure that's t' place tha wants, Miss?"

"Perfectly sure. I was told it was in or near Keighley, but I believe it may be actually in Oxenhope."

The address on Mary's letter had been Keighley, but she guessed that the mails were collected in the larger town. In that surmise she was apparently right for the waiter nodded.

"Aye, Keighley's main district town for all towns round here. Tha's not be wanting to be riding theer this day?"

"Indeed I'm hoping to ride there," she responded pleasantly. "Can you give me exact directions?"

"If thee turns back on't road, tha'll see a path winding ower t'moor," he said, having paused again. "Morton Grange is on't moor, not far from Leeshaw. But tha'd do better not t'think of riding so far."

"I shall enjoy it," she said briskly and went out to where Pegasus was tethered.

The horse gave her a reproachful look as she mounted up, clearly being of the same opinion as the waiter.

She had previously ridden past the path without noticing particularly where it wound and twisted between bracken that waved golden tips in the wind sweeping down the valley.

Beyond the bracken the turf was sparse, interrupted by patches of stony ground. The moor was crisscrossed at this place by low, drystone walls that followed the lie of the land, partnered by ditches whose trickles of water gave promise of streams when the rains came.

On the skyline stood a solitary farmhouse, its grey, ivied walls defying the elements.

Lilac rode towards that farmhouse, her expectations heightening. This must surely be the place, for she could discern no other buildings near. The gates were locked. Dismounting, she stared with disappointment at the yard beyond the bars. The facade of the house was bleak despite the ivy: the windows shuttered, the paintwork faded. It looked as if nobody had lived there for a very long time.

She had the definite impression this had never been a welcoming house. There was an air of disapproval about the tightly shuttered windows. The gate was both barred and padlocked as if the entire building were warning visitors to keep away. It was only her fancy, no doubt, but it occurred to Lilac that this silent and deserted dwelling place knew who she was and because of that knowledge, repelled her. On the gate the iron twisted into the name Morton Grange, and at each side the walls rose sheer and secretive. She began to walk slowly and thoughtfully round the outside of those forbidding walls, in search of another gate, but the only one she found was also locked. Small wonder that her mother had written that this seemed like the end of the world.

She was not certain exactly when she first became aware that someone was watching her. Unseen eyes followed as she continued to walk; and she was conscious of a prickling at the back of her neck—a sensation of unease. It had to be no more than imagination, but as she turned her head she could have sworn she caught a glimpse of a gap between shutter and window on the upper storey.

It was deathly quiet here with only the whistling of the wind and the sound of the horse's hooves on the bare earth. A pebble, dislodged by the wind, fell behind her and she jumped violently. She told herself it was fruitless to stay here when she could find out elsewhere who the current occupants might be.

She could, of course, raise her voice and shout. The owner would come to the door, apologising, "We don't get many visitors round these parts, so we're a mite cautious." However, Lilac could not bring herself to shout. There was no way of knowing who or what might emerge from that frowning porch.

A rook stirred skyward from the high slate roof of the

farmhouse and covered its threat to any who dared disturb its territory. Lilac mounted with more speed than grace and kicked Pegasus into something resembling a canter. The horse, too surprised to protest, took off at a fair pace, with Lilac feeling more and more thankful as the distance between herself and Morton Grange widened. By the time she slowed Pegasus to a walk the farmhouse was toy-sized in the distance, crouched below her in the valley. The absence of smoke from any of the chimneys persuaded her that she had merely given way to an irrational impulse of fear.

"And you were ready to journey all the way to India," she chided herself aloud.

Just then Pegasus stumbled suddenly and stood stock still, head hanging. Lilac slid from the saddle and studied him with concern to find out what might be the problem, but there seemed to be nothing. Yet, when she led him forward a few steps, he favoured his right foreleg slightly.

It looked like she would have to walk. The sensible thing would be to go back and find out if there was anybody at Morton Grange, but that sensible thing required more courage than she possessed at that moment. Even if she rode down to the road it would be an impossibly long walk home.

On the other hand she had obviously travelled here in a semi-circle, and it made even better sense to cut across the moor and approach Sladen Hall by way of the unweeded grounds at the rear of the house. A high outcropping of rocks ahead of her could also be seen from Sladen Hall, so if she walked in their direction she need only go round them to find herself where she wanted to be.

"Come on, Pegasus." She spoke cheerfully, deliberately careful not looking down at Morton Grange again.

Before she rode this way again, she would find out if the house was truly unoccupied; and, if not, who lived there and peeped out of shuttered windows. As for now, however, the ground was uneven and Pegasus slow. Lilac tried not to force the pace and felt a twinge of guilt at having pushed the poor old animal past his customary speed. He probably hadn't been ridden in years and was now lamed through her own stupidity.

The sun went in as abruptly as if it were offended. Lilac shivered, and the wind nipped the tips of her ears. The way was longer than she had anticipated. Distances were deceptive in this expanse of turf and heather and patches of peat bog. She had already skirted several of them, and the high rocks ahead were now more to her left . . . or was it right? Lilac felt a sudden chill, not caused by the wind, as she realised that what she had registered vaguely as a dark mass of cliff far ahead was actually a bank of black clouds rolling in, its edges trailing on the ground, its mass growing as the wind urged it nearer.

The sky had altered mood. Blue retreated into grey shot through with livid flashes. There was no rain; but she could hear the first, faint growling of approaching thunder. That weather could change so dramatically within the space of a few minutes seemed impossible. The landscape was changing as well. The far horizon was now obscured by the mist that hung like sable curtains between herself and the high crags.

Suddenly Lilac found herself ankle-deep in a patch of mud. She slithered clumsily for an instant on the edge of another peat bog that seemed to have sprung up from nowhere on purpose to trap her. She wrenched her feet free of the clinging, black stuff then stepped backwards and almost cannoned into Pegasus who whinnied a high, frightened note. The mist was all around Lilac now: dirty white at its fringes, black hearted. A fork of lightning split the sky a moment before the rain poured down.

There had to be shelter somewhere. Lilac began to skirt yet another patch of bog, moving one step at a time, telling herself firmly that this was only a summer storm and would quickly pass.

Meanwhile, the rain ran down her face, blurring her

vision along with the stifling mist, as the wind blew long ribbons of darkness towards her.

A shape loomed up in front of her. She put out her hand and touched stone. It was wall and with a gate which yielded to her frantic push. Straight ahead lights shone, glinting through the dark; and another flash of lightning illumined the outlines of a large house.

Houses and lights meant people. Lilac stumbled up the driveway and groped for a bell, seizing the rope more by luck than judgement and setting furiously a clang. The door opened. Lilac ducked beneath the lintel and stood, shaking the water from her eyes, as a voice demanded from within, "Who is it, John?"

"A young lass, sir, and a horse," the man who had admitted her called back.

"The devil it is." Quick footsteps sounded, and Chance Harland appeared in a nearby doorway.

"How d'ye do, Miss Morton? Pleasant afternoon for a social call," he observed.

"I was out riding," Lilac said haughtily, "and my horse went lame."

"You're not riding Pegasus?" he exclaimed.

"He stumbled over a stone, I think. I cannot think he was hurt badly, but he is favouring his leg a lot," she said, somewhat breathlessly as the fact that she had arrived at Chance Harland's house penetrated her confusion.

"Nathan." He raised his voice to shout, and a thick-set man, his sleeves rolled up, came in from the back of the hall.

"If he might be stabled?" Lilac said diffidently. "The leg may require a poultice."

"The only thing old Pegasus requires is a good groom and a thorough scolding," Chance informed her. "Nathan, see to it. Going lame is one of Pegasus's favourite tricks when he decides that he's had sufficient exercise for the day. You'd best come to the fire before you catch a cold. I've no doubt that you're as nesh as most city folk."

"What on earth is 'nesh'?" she demanded.

"A local word," he told her, "meaning spineless."

Well! That was the worst insult Lilac had ever received. She opened her lips to reply furiously but, instead, found herself propelled into a spacious chamber with a log fire burning on an enormous hearth.

"Get your clothes off," Chance ordered.

"I will do no such thi—"

"I'm leaving the room," he interrupted with a decidedly malicious grin that made him more than ever resemble a fox. "I will toss in some clean clothes for you and be certain to keep my eyes closed to spare your blushes. Otherwise, you may perish of cold, if such is your wish. In which case, I'd be obliged if you would leave immediately since I have a superstitious dislike of dead bodies on the premises."

The door closed behind him before she could think of a suitably quelling answer, leaving Lilac to glare at the unoffending panels as she removed her wet garments and draped them over the backs of the nearby chairs. She had reached her chemise, which seemed dry enough to retain, when an arm appeared round the edge of the reopening door and flung a bundle of garments onto the carpet at her feet.

"I'll get you something hot to drink," Chance's voice announced as the door closed once more.

The dress he'd given her was designed for a woman six inches taller and three inches wider than Lilac. She tied the sash as tightly as she could and folded over the low neckline, wondering what manner of woman chose bright orange with a pink stripe running through it and what such a dress was doing in a bachelor establishment anyway.

There was a towel with the bundle. She used it to rub her head vigorously, hoping she would not resemble too hoydenish a female when she had finished. Meanwhile, the warmth was stealing back into her limbs, and her sense of panic had diminished. That she had turned up on the doorstep of an ill-bred neighbour was unlucky, but it was preferable to being lost on the moor in a thunderstorm.

"I assume you are fit to be seen now," said Chance upon his return. In his hand was a tall, silver pitcher of something from which steam rose. He passed it to her.

"Thank you, Mr Harland." Anything further she might have had in mind to say was lost in a fit of choking as the scalding liquid burned her throat.

"My, but you're quite a tippler, aren't you?" he observed. "Most ladies sip."

"What in the world is in this?" Lilac mopped her streaming eyes.

"A concoction of my own of whisky, lemons, nutmeg, oatmeal, honey, and ginger," he said.

"I never drank whisky before." Lilac sipped more cautiously at the brew and was agreeably surprised as the burning in her throat became a glow.

"You may develop a taste for it," he said. "I take it that you won't refuse something to eat as well? Drinking on an empty stomach isn't to be advised."

"I really don't mean to be an inconvenience," she began.

"Nonsense, women delight in making themselves inconvenient," he retorted. "I believe they take lessons in it at school. Now, why don't you sit down and we'll dry your feet."

She sat down weakly. He knelt and pulled off her muddy boots.

"Fortunately, you don't appear to have completely ruined my carpet. Where's the towel?"

"On the floor," Lilac answered.

The sight of Chance Harland stripping away her wringing wet stockings and briskly rubbing her feet and ankles tempted her to giggle, but she resisted.

"So you were riding on the moor? Anywhere in particular?" he asked, glancing up at her.

If he could conceal the fact that he had once lived in

Sladen Hall, then she could hide the purpose of her expedition, thought Lilac.

"I was merely exploring," she said airily, swallowing a hiccough.

"Without a groom? You are an unconventional creature, aren't you? Or were you hoping for an adventure?"

"If you are implying that I deliberately got myself lost in order to force myself upon you," she said stiffly, "I do assure you, sir, that nothing was further from my thoughts. Had I known it was your home I would have . . . I would have continued on my way without stopping."

"And lost the opportunity of displaying your pretty ankles?" He raised an eyebrow.

Lilac tried to think of a reply that would crush him utterly, but found to her horror that she was once again to giggle.

"You are a trifle miffed, Miss Morton," said Chance, rising and staring down at her with an expression of wry amusement on his harsh features. "I must get some food inside you before my reputation suffers. Excuse me."

He went out again, leaving her there in the borrowed dress as the big, warm chamber began to whirl dizzily round.

= 10 =

THE STORM STILL raged outside, but within the sound of the thunder was muted and heavy curtains kept out the lightning flashes. Another manservant, as casually dressed as Nathan had been, set supper on a round table near the fire and withdrew. Perhaps he was accustomed to seeing small, young ladies in too-big clothes sitting in his employer's chair and sipping the dregs of a lethal whisky mixture from a silver pitcher.

"When you have eaten something you will begin to sober up." Chance had returned and was piling food onto a plate.

"I was never intoxicated in my entire life," Lilac said with dignity.

"Until now." He cocked an eyebrow at her. "You must not fear that I'll think you a soak, for it's clear you have a weak head for alcohol. How old are you?"

"I will be eighteen in a short time."

"Yes, of course." He put the heaped plate on a smaller table at her elbow. "I might have worked that out."

"I am surprised you did not," she commented. "Since you are so quick at figuring."

"How did you know that?"

"Your exercise books are still at Sladen Hall." Finding herself hungry, she began to eat.

"The devil they are. I had forgotten."

"As you had doubtless forgotten that you once lived there."

"I hadn't forgotten. I simply didn't think it worth the mentioning."

"But you did live there?" She was curious, watching a shadow flit across his face.

"When I was a child. My parents died, and my grandfather decided that I'd benefit from company. So I came here only at weekends and spent my weeks at Sladen Hall with Mark."

"Mark?"

"Mark Sladen. His parents were still alive. He was the only son. The arrangement suited all parties concerned. My grandfather had to put up with a small boy for only two days a week, and I received some kind of education."

"Then Mark's parents died too?"

"It's an inconvenient habit people have," he said dryly. "My grandfather had also shuffled off this mortal coil. So I returned here, having imbibed as much learning as I intended, and took up my duties as local squire. I saw little of Mark Sladen after that. He was killed at Trafalgar. The damn fool volunteered in the hope of becoming a hero and achieved his ambition. Unfortunately, being dead, he couldn't enjoy it. I hope you don't object to cold pheasant. I don't usually trouble much with a formal repast in the evenings."

"Surely it is not yet evening?" Lilac exclaimed.

"In Yorkshire we eat at six. We don't have sophisticated London habits. I don't intend to offer you wine. You may have a strong coffee."

"I am not still in the schoolroom," she said coldly.

"I reckon you only just closed the door behind you though." His sudden smile was unexpectedly charming. "Seventeen going on eighteen is not exactly elderly. Will you have fruit?"

Lilac shook her head. The dizziness was clearing now and her confidence returning.

"I will have to leave soon," she said, accepting coffee. "Alice will be frantic."

"Alice?"

"My maid. I brought her with me from London. She is setting the house to rights as it is impossible to live there in any degree of comfort in its present state."

"Since Alice allowed you to go riding without escort, she will take no harm from a few hours' fretting."

"It is I who command Alice."

"Then you are indeed unusual, for my servants keep me in strict subjection. They would not countenance my riding out on such a day."

"Storms don't last forever."

"By the time this one is done it will be completely dark, so you will have to accept my hospitality for the night."

"I couldn't possibly," she said in horror.

"There are eight bedrooms. You may have choice of any five of them."

Doing rapid calculations in her head, Lilac said, "Only two servants?"

"Nathan and John. Now and then a couple of women come over from Stanmore to clean, but I manage well enough."

"I couldn't possibly stay where there were no other women."

"You seem not to have been so squeamish when you were riding about on the moor."

"That was quite different," she protested.

"You mean that you will have no horse in your bedchamber on which to gallop away and thus escape my evil designs?"

He was laughing at her, but it was impossible to dislike him as much as she wished to.

"I am sure," she said uncertainly, "that you are a gentleman."

"Nonsense, you are not sure of anything of the kind. I can only say that you must have moved in some exceedingly degenerate society if the men you know are in the habit of taking advantage of unprotected schoolgirls."

"It is what people will say."

"When we announce it round the neighbourhood," he said amiably, "we will be sure to mention that you locked the door."

"It seems I have no choice," she said.

"Excellent. At last we agree on something. Now let me pour you another cup of coffee, and you will tell me when you intend to return to London."

"In about six months."

"That is idiocy." His voice was suddenly harsh again. "What can you possibly find to do in the wilds of Yorkshire during the winter? A lone girl with only three servants. You must have relatives other than your late grandmother who will take responsibility for you."

"I have an uncle—great-uncle rather—but he is in Africa."

"There must be friends or neighbours who would take care of you."

"I am quite old enough to take care of myself, thank you."

"So far you have not given very convincing evidence of that," he said dryly.

"Also I wished to find out something about my mother and father. My father was killed by savages, you know."

"By savages?"

"In America, where he went to preach the Gospel. You must have heard."

"I heard that both your parents were dead, and that the child had also died."

"I suppose my grandmother told them that—my Morton grandparents, I mean—because of the way they had treated my mother," Lilac mused.

"Then would it not be more honourable to abide by your grandmother's wishes?"

"I want to know more about my mother," she said earnestly. "My grandmother always said that she was very saintly and sweet, but I cannot see her plain as a real person."

"It is not necessary to know one's parents initmately in order to be aware of one's own identity."

"But you knew her," Lilac persisted. "You recognised me by my eyes. She must have made a great impression on you for your to remember that after more than seventeen years."

"I saw her now and then. She was extremely pretty. Sometimes she used to walk out on the moor. The Mortons must have been gloomy company at the best of times, and she was not yet nineteen."

"And my father?" Lilac blushed slightly as she remembered her mother's letter. Her father had disapproved of Chance Harland's profligate habits.

"I met him," Chance said now, and his tone was curt. "We were not friends."

"I have no likeness of him, only of my mother. What was he like?"

"Dark-haired, middle height, dark eyes. A woman would have called him handsome."

"But you did not?"

"I am not a woman. He seemed cold and cynical to me, forever ready to believe the worst of his fellow man. The evening is still young. I trust we are not going to spend it in talking about people you never knew and I had only the briefest acquaintanceship with."

"Morton Grange," Lilac said slowly. "I suppose it belongs to me now?"

"I'm sorry to disillusion you, but it was rented," Chance told her. "It used to be called High Farm, but the Mortons changed the name when they became tenants. The new name stuck. Is that where you were bound this afternoon?"

Again the sharpness in his voice. Lilac frowned, wanting to ask why, but contented herself with a vague reply.

"It might have been interesting to see the house where

my parents spent the first months of their married life before they went to the New World."

"It's a farmhouse like any other. I will escort you there myself one day," he said.

"That's very kind of you." She looked at him in astonishment, wondering what had caused his sudden change of attitude.

"You'll likely get lost again if you set out alone. Shall we say the day after tomorrow? I'll bring over a horse that won't give you a dramatic performance of lameness. Pegasus is the most intelligent horse I ever knew and the laziest."

"The day after tomorrow then," she said.

"That being settled how shall we amuse ourselves? You play the piano, of course."

"So badly that it would be poor return for your hospitality."

"How refreshing to hear you say that," he said and his face was charming again. "Most young ladies are only too anxious to display their lack of skill."

"You are hard on young ladies, sir."

"On missish ones, certainly. I find them tedious. Do you play cards?"

"Grandmother disapproved."

"And we had best not disturb her eternal rest. You were fond of her."

"Apart from Uncle Philip she was the only relative I had. We were not demonstratively affectionate, but I was fond of her, yes."

"Do you play billiards?"

"You don't have to think up ways of amusing me, you know," Lilac said.

"It is more to occupy my own time," Chance told her. "If we can find nothing to while away the evening, then I shall be strongly tempted to make love to you; and that would offend your sense of propriety. The truth is that you look extremely lovely in that hideous gown."

"Was it your mother's?"

"No, dear, it belonged to a mistress of mine who flounced out of my life and left a trunkful of clothes behind to remember her by."

"Oh," said Lilac, her voice faint, her cheeks flushing.

Never in her life had she heard anyone refer openly to a mistress. She was not even certain what the term implied, since Grandmother had informed her that the Good Lord sent babies. That was the reason for marriage. That there were women, unmentioned in polite society, who did not marry was a side of life about which Lilac had heard only the vaguest rumour. Staring at Chance Harland, she suddenly understood that what mistresses did had very little to do with the Good Lord.

"You really are a baby, aren't you?" he said, his voice and eyes gentling. "Come. Hitch up that ridiculously trailing skirt, and we'll play billiards. If you have never played, then you will enjoy it. They say that Cleopatra was an expert. I would not advise you to emulate her in her other pursuits, but you will come to no harm with a cue in your hand."

He opened the door and she followed him, still blushing, down a short passage to a panelled room dominated by a table covered in green baize.

"The object of the game is to get the balls into the pockets at the sides," he informed her.

"Is that all?"

"There are rules concerning the sequence and the number of shots taken; but yes, Miss Morton, basically that is all."

"I believe I can do that," Lilac said.

"First you will learn how to hold the cue correctly."

He came to her side, putting the slender stick into her hands, arranging her fingers and arms. His hip pressed against hers in a way she tried vainly to ignore. He smelt of bay and lemon; and over and above tht was another scent—strange, exciting, male.

"Are you sure this is a respectable game?" she asked cautiously.

"Quite sure, my child. Now, let us see how many shots you require to pot that ball into that pocket."

He stood back as he spoke and leaned against the wall, chalking another cue.

Lilac bent over the edge of the table, measured the distance with her eye and potted the ball.

"Beginner's luck," Chance said. "Try for that one."

"It seems a rather pointless game to me," Lilac remarked, potting a second and a third ball.

Chance had begun to laugh. She missed the next shot and turned reproachful eyes on him.

"Perhaps you had better tell me the rules, sir, as I am clearly doing something wrong."

"Miss Morton, you have hidden talents. Remind me never to play against you for money," he said, still chuckling. "Now I will tell you the ground rules; and, since you are clearly a natural, we will play with no quarter given."

He had obviusly played often and in the end proved the winner by a narrow margin. His eyes danced as he bowed and took the cue from her.

"You are indeed a worthy opponent, Miss Morton. I shall grant you a return game sometime, but now I think you ought to retire to your chamber."

"Is the storm over?"

"Come and look for yourself."

He drew back the curtains, and she gazed out into a calm darkness. The steady dripping of rain from the eaves was the only sound.

"Perhaps it would be possible for me to get home after all," she suggested.

"There's no moon, and the moor will be treacherous with the beck probably flooded again. I have already told Nathan to make the room ready. I believe it is the chamber that you would have chosen for yourself. Follow me."

He opened the door gain and led her up a short flight of

stairs to a landing from which a corridor stretched with doors opening off it.

"I fear that if you are afflicted with the nightmare in the middle of the night," Chance said solemnly, "your cries won't be heard. I sleep at the other end of the house, as do John and Nathan."

"I don't get nightmares," Lilac assured him.

"Then I wish you a peaceful night, Miss Morton. He stood aside and allowed her to pass into the lamplit room before bowling again and walking off down the stairs.

The bedchamber was not large but it was comfortable. A fire was burning and reflected the gleam of polished wood and silver candelabra. The bed had been made and the curtains drawn across.

There was a nightgown laid out across the bed. Lilac stared at it, resolving that she would keep on her borrowed dress. The situation was an unusual one in all conscience, but she drew the line at wearing a nightgown which had belonged to Chance Harland's mistress.

She stepped to the window and pulled back the curtain. Outside, the last of the rain dripped past the window; and, though there was no moon, there were stars glinting through the dark. She fancied she could discern the high, rocky outline of the crags. If so, then she had not been very far out of her way after all.

She wished that Chance had been willing to tell her more about her parents. She was quite certain there was more to tell. His manner had been so abrupt and hostile when she made enquiry. Her father had admonished him for his behaviour—the wild conduct of a youth not yet twenty. Perhaps her father, with his ambitions to be a missionary, had been a trifle priggish about the sowing of wild oats indulged in by his neighbour. On the other hand, there was the vivid dress with its low neckline that she had so modestly folded over and the nightgown on the bed. It looked as if Chance Harland hadn't reformed even after he had grown up.

There was a bolt on the inside of the door. She drew it softly and wondered if he might come, sort-footed to try it during the night. He had made clear that he considered her to be a schoolgirl, but one never could be too careful when dealing with the masculine sex. Lilac knew that from her reading of current novels. Men had one thought in their minds. The books she read never specified what that thought was, but she was beginning to glean a hazy notion.

When the knock did come on her door she almost jumped out of her skin with fright. She had been expecting something and, impelled by her own imagination, it had happened.

"Yes?" She crossed to the door and stood tensely.

"The nightgown belonged to my mother," came Chance Harland's voice. "I feel sure you will not object to wearing it."

"No, of course not," she said loudly.

"Your own garments will be left at the door in the morning," the voice continued. "I have to go out early on business so you will probably be gone by the time I return."

"You've been very kind," Lilac said, and wondered why on earth she should feel a sinking sense of disappointment in her stomach.

"The day after tomorrow I'll call for you at ten," he said." You can take a look at Morton Grange though I warn you there is nothing to see."

"Good-night, Mr. Harland," she said politely.

"Good-night, Miss Morton."

His voice was equally polite, but she detected a note of amusement in it. There was something uncanny in the way he had divined her squeamishness about the nightgown. Certainly it betokened a knowledge of the workings of the feminine mind that was a trifle alarming. As she prepared to disrobe Lilac couldn't help wondering what sort of nightgown his mistress had worn.

=11=

"I SHALL NEVER get over the shock of it, miss. Never."

"You must have realised that I'd take shelter somewhere," Lilac protested.

"I 'ad visions of you stuck fast and drowned dead in a bog," Alice continued unheeding. "It would 'ave been my fault. I 'adn't ought to 'ave let you ride off by yourself."

"Well, as you may see, I'm perfectly all right," Lilac said. "Mr. Harland was most helpful and courteous."

"The point is," Alice said darkly, " 'as 'e offered marriage?"

"For goodness sake, Alice, you speak as if I had been compromised."

"Ruined is more like," Alice said. "Even if you 'aven't it's only common decency."

"Mr Harland regards me as a child, Alice, and a rather troublesome child at that. He certainly wouldn't regard what happened as in any way hurtful to my reputation."

"I thought they 'ad a funny way of looking at things in Yorkshire," Alice said, only slightly mollified. "I only pray they don't get to 'ear of it back 'ome, that's all."

Lilac felt rather relieved that she had not confided about the dress she had worn while her own clothes were being dried. She had given the impression that she had reached Chance Harland's house before the storm had fully broken. Alice was being ridiculous, of course, since he was in his late thirties and not likely to be interested in a girl of seventeen. That last thought was unaccountably depressing. Lilac shrugged it away and went off to wash her hair and decide what she was going to wear the following day.

She had not seen her host again when she woke up that morning. A tap on the door and Nathan's dour voice had informed her that her clothes were ready and so was breakfast, to be served in the room where they sat the previous evening. By daylight, the house was revealed as a building of moderate size and undoubted taste, the interior luxuriously furnished and seeming to proclaim that a man did not require a wife in order to live in a civilised fashion. Nathan escorted her to the end of the drive and pointed out the path that would bring her out close to Sladen Hall, and Pegasus had strolled home with no more than an occasional limp when he forgot for a moment that his act had been found out.

Tomorrow she would behave in a completely grown-up manner, Lilac resolved, and make such comments as would lead Chance Harland to regard her as an intelligent female and not a ninny.

For the rest of this day, however, she remained within doors helping Alice to mend the linen, a task Lilac disliked and performed very badly but one which occupied her attention from straying to an image of Amelia as a radiant bride.

The next morning the sun shone as if it were making up for lost time, and Lilac felt a decided sense of anticipation as she donned her riding habit and sat down to wait for Chance Harland.

Alice, to her amusement, had offered no objections to the ride.

"After a night at 'is 'ouse, a ride in broad daylight seems respectable," she said. "If you takes care to stay in the saddle."

He arrived shortly after ten, mounted on a black stallion and leading a pretty mare.

"Her name is Daisy," he told Lilac who had gone out to

meet him. "You are welcome to have the use of her while you are here."

"Will you come in, sir, and take something before we go?" she asked.

"I'd prefer to start at once lest the weather changes suddenly. At this season it's not to be relied upon, and I've business later in the day."

A neat way of informing her that she need not count on a lengthy expedition, thought Lilac as she mounted up. She glimpsed Alice's head at an upper window and frowned warningly.

"Your servant is inspecting me and will doubtless give an opinion when you return," Chance said.

"Alice is apt to forget that I am no longer a child," Lilac said, flushing.

"At least you had the good sense to bring her. Come." He wheeled about and set a good pace down the drive.

The landscape sparkled with a million raindrops caught on every blade of grass, and tiny jets of water streamed upwards as the horses trotted over them. The wind was keen, bringing a glow to Lilac's face and tugging at the strings of her riding hat.

"You did not mention that you had ridden past Morton Grange already," he said abruptly.

"How did—?"

"Somebody saw you. You came from the Oxenhope road."

"The old farmhouse was Morton Grange?" Lilac said.

"You were not aware of it?" He sent her a slanting look. "I daresay the name was not writ large enough on the gates."

Her cheeks burning she rode on, wondering who had told him. Perhaps the unseen watcher she sensed had noticed her hesitation.

"The three houses are set in a triangle," he said seeming not to mark her confusion. "The crags act as the balancing point between them. Sladen Hall, Morton Grange, and my own place."

"How is your house called?"

"Harland House. My great-grandfather built it. He and the Sladens were friends. At one time there was talk of marriage between the children on each side, but nothing came of it. It might have been the start of a rural dynasty. As it is, Mark died unwed, and his property passed to distant relatives who have no links with the neighbourhood. For my part, I am a contented bachelor."

"Mrs Watson says that no bachelor is contented," Lilac said.

"And who is Mrs Watson?"

"She is the mother of my best friend, Amelia. At least she was my best friend, but now she is marrying and will sail soon to India."

"You are not attending your best friend's nuptials?"

"I am in mourning," Lilac said primly.

The bronze eyes turned to rove over her dark green habit and the jaunty feather of gold stuck in her hat.

"Yes, I do see," Chance said. "Obviously you cannot go out and about in society at all at present. To whom is your former best friend plighting her troth?"

"To a lieutenant in the regiment."

"Does he have a name or shall we while away the time by guessing?"

"Wentworth—Peter Wentworth."

"No doubt an estimable young man, full of zeal for foreign service. We are approaching Morton Grange, but nobody takes this route as a general rule. There are several patches of peat bog so, unless one knows the area, there is a certain danger in wandering across it without due care."

They were riding down the slope now towards the farmhouse. Being with someone made a difference. The nervousness that had troubled her previously had gone, though the house still had a bleak and unwelcoming aspect.

As they rode up to the gates, Lilac uttered an exclamation of surprise. They were open.

"There's a caretaker," Chance told her. "He comes over from time to time and checks on the house. I persuaded him to let me have carte blanche in viewing it."

It must have been the caretaker who had watched her ride past. Her own imagination had supplied the sinister atmosphere.

"There's furniture." She gave another exclamation as he fitted a key into the front door which swung open to reveal a large chamber with oak settles and a long table.

"It was let furnished."

"To my grandparents? Who took it after them?"

"There have been no tenants since."

"Surely that's unusual." Lilac began to walk round slowly. The apartment was clean, so the caretaker obviously did his task properly.

"It's a fairly isolated situation," Chance said. "Not many are willing to bury themselves in such a spot."

"And my grandparents died ten years ago?"

"Something like that. I was never exactly on visiting terms with them."

"Would you mind if I were to go round by myself?" she asked.

"I'll wait outside. If you're planning on turning this into a sentimental pilgrimage I would remind you that your mother, on the few occasions I saw her, never looked particularly pleased to be living here."

He gave a curt nod and stepped out into the yard again, where the horses were tethered.

This was an old house, she thought, beginning to explore. The front door opened directly into what had clearly been the main living quarters. The fireplace was immense and the furniture had the heavy carving of a previous century. In the far corner a narrow flight of stairs rose to the upper floor and two doors in the adjacent wall led into what had been parlour and pantry. The family would have sat in the main room during the evenings. Or perhaps her parents had the use of the tiny parlour. There were no pictures on the walls, only a framed motto "Thou God Seest Me", over the fireplace.

Lilac climbed the narrow stairs that twisted at the top onto a landing with five doors opening from it. Up here the place was dustier, with the stale smell of a house long unoccupied.

The books were in a neat row at the head of the stairs, their spines proclaiming their title. She tilted her head, reflecting that Foxe's *Martyrs*, and *Collected Sermons* of William Grimshaw seemed to be the livliest reading matter the Morgans had possessed.

In the small bedrooms there were high beds with wooden posts but no draperies of any kind, and chairs and cupboards flush with the walls. The windows were shuttered. She tugged one shutter open and looked down into the yard. Chance Harland was out on the moor beyond the high walls that surrounded the yard. The morning sun gleamed gold on the red of his bent head. He seemed to be in a brown study, walking slowly and pensively.

The room held no memories. She was not sure in which chamber her parents had slept, for they were all exactly alike: the walls panelled, the complete absence of drapes or ornament lending them a bleak aspect. It was possible that the ornaments and pictures had all been stored away, but she had the distinct impression that when the Mortons lived here the house had been equally bare. It was small wonder her mother had looked sad when she walked out on the moor.

She opened one or two of the cupboards, but they were empty. The expedition had yielded nothing, not even a pleasantly sentimental nostalgia. She went down the stairs again and into the main room. The place was cold even though the day was warm. Her mother must have hated it. When she emerged from the house Chance was just returning from his stroll on the moor. His expression was still pensive and she wondered why.

"You saw what you wished to see?" He gave her a strained smile.

"The house has only furniture in it," she said.

"It's a long time since anyone lodged there. Neither is it always a happy idea to try to resurrect the past," he said.

"I suppose not." She watched him as he fitted the key into the lock, then asked impulsively, "Who owns the property? You said the Mortons rented it."

"My grandfather bought it from a family called Rolfe who were emigrating."

"Your grand—? Then you are now the owner?"

"It appears so." He pocketed the key and started towards his mount.

"But why didn't you say so?" Lilac asked in bewilderment.

"You didn't ask before," he said.

"Then my grandparents paid rent to your grandfather?"

"To the land agent. Relations between the Mortons and Grandfather were not exactly cordial."

"You didn't say," she repeated.

"It can hardly be a matter of pressing importance to you who owns the house, since nobody you are connected with lives there now," he observed.

"I suppose not," she said unwillingly.

"And as you have found there is nothing there to excite your interest." He had come to help her up to the saddle.

"I hoped I might feel some sense of Mama's presence," she confessed, "but there was nothing. I wish you had known her better."

"I'm afraid I can tell you no more than I've told you already," he said, mounting up himself. "The relations between our two households were never cordial. My grandfather had just died and I'd taken over at Harland House. I was eighteen and not very responsive to lectures on morality from my neighbours. I went up to Scotland to stay with some friends in the autumn, and by the time I returned your parents were no longer in the district."

"They went to America," Lilac said. "My father must have been killed almost immediately, and my mother returned to London."

"I assume that is what your grandmother told you, your maternal grandmother, I mean?"

Lilac nodded, glancing back over her shoulder to the bleak farmhouse crouching in its hollow. Barbara had spoken little about practical matters concerned with her daughter's marriage. She had talked only of the high calling of a missionary and of Mary's angelic nature.

"Now that you have satisfied your curiosity you will be returning south, I daresay?" Chance spoke casually but she caught again the strained expression on his harsh face.

"I cannot imagine why you should assume that," she said. "I rented Sladen Hall for six months."

"Under a false name, which seems rather a pointless thing to do."

"Only the first name, and I told you the reason for that." She spoke sharply, wishing he wouldn't make it quite so obvious that he wanted her gone. "I fancied the Mortons might still be alive and that there might have been some misunderstanding in the family to explain why they never tried to contact me, but they were not apparently told I had survived. It seems an extraordinary thing for my grandmother to have done."

"The Mortons might have claimed you," he said, "and reared you to be a little missionary."

"That was in very bad taste," she reproached. "You forget my father died for the Christian faith, sir."

"So I did," he agreed, apparently unrepentant. "As I told you I was in Scotland at the time."

"And, as I have rented Sladen Hall for six months, I intend to stay."

"There is precious little social life in the district," he warned, "except for the occasional carouse at my house, of course; and I hardly think that Alice would approve of your attending one of those. You are not yet out and so cannot go to the York Balls, even if it is possible in our dreadful winters to travel that far."

"Then I shall spend a quiet winter overseeing the renovation of the house and grounds."

"You are an obstinate young woman, I see." His smile was down-curving. "If you linger in the depths of the country for too long, all the young officers will have sailed to India, you know?"

"Heavens, sir, I am not interested in officers." She spoke with great hauteur, her face crimsoning. "I do assure you that I have not the faintest interest in the comings and goings of the military."

"Did your best friend, Amelia, steal away your beau?" he enquired.

That was so near the truth that she winced, her bright colour fading. Chance, shooting her a sideways glance, observed, "You are not cut out to be an adventuress, Miss Morton. You have too transparent a face. I advise you to go home. Rummaging in the past of two people that you never knew will prove a most boring occupation. I promise you. As for renovating the Sladen place, it has been neglected for so many years that a few more can make no difference."

"Do you have any more advice for me?" she enquired sweetly.

"Only that you confine your riding to gentle jaunts within sight of Sladen Hall," he said.

"I fail to see by what right—."

"I am lending you Daisy until you return to London. I treat my animals well and have no desire to see her lamed in a bog or chilled because you get yourself lost in another mist."

He still thought her a stupid child. She would have loved to tell him haughtily that he could take back his loan; but, if she did that, she would only have old Pegasus to ride.

"I will take very good care of Daisy," she said at last, her voice shaking with muted rage.

"Ride only near the house. I am not always at home to waifs and strays."

"And clearly too busy to have time to spare for neighbours," she snapped. "I shall wish you good morning, sir, as I can see the gates of Sladen Hall from here. I doubt if even I can get lost between here and there."

She didn't wait for his answer but spurred Daisy on without a backward glance.

=== 12 ===

NEVER IN HER entire life had she met a more unpredictable man, Lilac decided as she walked in the garden later in the day. Chance Harland lent her a horse and then made it impossible for her to ride far afield. He had gone to the trouble of showing her over Morton Grange, then pestered her into telling him when she was leaving the district with as much persistence as if her being there were a personal inconvenience to him.

Worst of all, he had practically guessed she had fled to Yorkshire to forget a disappointment in love. The humiliation of that made her burn with temper all over again. She told herself firmly that his opinion wasn't worth a jot and walked on towards the lilac garden. The blossoms were fading now as autumn crept on, their petals browning at the edges, their leaves tattering like lace in the wind that gusted through the tangled weeds and creepers. Yet the perfume lingered, hovering at the corners of her mind even as she was thinking about other things.

She would remain for the winter just to annoy Chance Harland. Already Sladen Hall was presenting a more attractive aspect to the eye, with the floors waxed, the drapes washed, the chill gone from rooms where fires has been lit, and the books neatly arranged in the tall bookcases. The Sladens had a cheerful taste in literature at least, she reflected, recalling the gloomy volumes ranged at the head of the stairs in Morton Grange. Several of the books at Sladen Hall had the name Mark Sladen written on their fly leaves. He had been Chance Harland's friend, had shared lessons with him, and been killed at Trafalgar, and had probably known her mother too.

It was a pity that he was no longer available for her to talk with and find out more than she had found out so far. Chance had implied there was nothing more to know, but Lilac sensed a puzzle growing as she ran through the meagre facts already at her disposal.

The Mortons had been as far as she could tell grim and gloomy people, disapproving of the most innocent vanities; and their son, Robert, had been filled with missionary zeal.

Her mother had been unhappy during her stay in Yorkshire. Frightened, Lilac reminded herself. It had been clearly stated in the letter dated September. In the four months between the writing of that letter and Lilac's own birth the younger Mortons had sailed to America, her father had been killed, and Mary had returned to London to give birth to Lilac and die.

"Grandmother told the Mortons that the baby had died too," Lilac said aloud and sat down on a fallen tree stump, her chin cupped in her hands, to ponder the matter. To have done such a thing didn't sound like her grandmother at all, even if the Mortons had been unpleasant people. Barbara Lameter had been an honourable lady. Whatever her private sentiments, she would not have concealed the birth of a living child from a couple whose only son had been killed by savages. It simply didn't make sense.

That evening Lilac had the piles of exercise and account books brought to her in the parlour and set herself the task of going through them. The account books were fascinating. She had not realised how steeply prices had risen since the wars with France began. The exercise books were a mixture of various subjects. Chance Harland and Mark Sladen had apparently drawn fairly equal grades in their studies. Flicking through Latin declensions and irregular verbs, Lilac smiled wryly as she pictured two small boys longing to go out and play. Now one small boy was dead in battle, and the other lad grown into a harsh and contradictory individual.

That night she dreamed of lilacs, lush and sensuous, their blossoms spilling over into her lap and their perfume heavy in her nostrils. Then she raised her face to Lieutenant Peter Wentworth for a kiss, and he had eyes the colour of bronze and hair like the pelt of a fox. She sat bolt upright in bed, wakeful and cross. It was not yet dawn but she found it impossible to think of sleep again. The fire in the hearth had fallen into glowing cinders, and the air had a chill.

She reached for dressing gown and slippers and padded across the freshly polished floor towards the window. The curtains were drawn across, and, when she parted them, she was looking out into a grey mist of tree and wall. Not even the birds were awake yet. In London one grew accustomed to the street noises, but the absence of noise was equally disturbing.

Someone was below in the garden. Filled with a sudden, unreasoning nervousness, she let the curtain fall and peeped through the chink that was left. It was Elijah, probably rousing himself to go to the stables where he had Daisy as well to look after now. However, it was not Elijah, unless he had grown several inches and dyed his hair.

Chance Harland passed beneath her window, his head bent, without even glancing up. He was walking up the drive now, which meant his mount had been left at the gate. Why? The question wouldn't be answered by hiding behind the window curtains. Lilac opened her door and stepped out into the corridor. She could hear the sound of Alice's rhythmic snoring from her chamber.

There was a light footstep on the stair at the point where it twisted onto the landing. Lilac stepped back, pushing the door close, as Fanny came up the stairs, a shawl over her head and a satisfied smile on her face. She went towards her own room without turning, jingling something softly in her hand. Lilac heard the clink of coin just before Fanny closed the door.

Chance Harland and Fanny? The possibilities that thought opened up were disturbing and . . . disgusting. Lilac sat down on the end of her bed and scowled. Fanny was a servant girl and a slattern. It simply didn't seem possible that a fastidious man like Chance Harland would even consider a girl like Fanny. Lilac reminded herself that she knew nothing of his life beyond the little he'd elected to tell her. And there was the dress she herself had been obliged to borrow. He had admitted shamelessly that it belonged to a mistress of his. Lilac had imagined some elegant, if rather colourful woman, not a servant who had to be chivvied to do her work. Perhaps that was why she and her brother stayed on at Sladen Hall.

"And I," whispered Lilac aloud, "stayed a night alone in the house of such a man."

This discovery released her from any obligation to keep her promise to ride near the house. She was now determined to ride where she pleased and to stay in Yorkshire as long as she chose. In fact, she would ride that very day into Keighley and make enquiries as to where her grandparents were buried. It was likely their graves hadn't been kept up, and she owed them that duty at least.

If Chance Harland had behaved in such a fashion while her parents were staying in Morton Grange she was not surprised that her father had remonstrated. She was even beginning to feel a sneaking sympathy for the Mortons' point of view.

"If you get lost again don't go blaming me," Alice warned with resignation in her voice as she watched Lilac mount up. "You won't be told, will you, Miss?"

"That's right, Alice. I'm obstinate and stubborn," Lilac said lightly. "I shall take my meal in Keighley and if there is the faintest sign of a break in the weather I will hire a guide to see me safely home."

"I wish we was 'ome," Alice said gloomily. "I can't stir

Fanny this morning to move faster than a snail. She looks tired to death. Never worked so 'ard for years, I don't expect."

Fanny had tired herself out with pleasure not work, Lilac thought. She had a sudden vision of the servant, shawl slipping from her curly head, in the strong arms of Chance Harland.

It was such an unpleasant image that she hastily separated them in her mind and rode down the drive at a pace which startled even the lively Daisy.

It had begun to look as if all the men she ever fell in love with were destined to be interested in other women, she thought gloomily.

Lilac pulled Daisy up short, staring ahead with her mouth opening in astonishment. There must be something wrong with her. It was less than a month since her heart had been broken by Lieutenant Peter Wentworth. Now, here she was, jealous of a servant girl when she didn't even like Chance Harland. He was a rake, she told herself irritably, and had never given the faintest sign of even admiring her.

"I don't want him to admire me," she said aloud and jerked the reins to urge Daisy toward a pace that would render thinking difficult.

She reached Keighley without mishap; and, by the time she stabled the mare, had convinced herself that she had not the slightest interest in the private carryings on of Mr Chance Harland. What she was suffering from was reaction. Girls who had been disappointed in love frequently rushed into the arms of the nearest man on the rebound; and, save for a brief moment when he had shown her how to hold the billiard cue, she hadn't actually been in his arms at all.

Meanwhile, her best course of action was to enquire at the parish church about the whereabouts of the graves of the Mortons. There would be a register there, she supposed. They had died ten years before, Chance Harland said. There had been moments during their ride together when she could have fancied admiration in his eyes. Not that it made a particle of difference to her dislike of him, and she was probably mistaken anyway. After all, she had been certain that the lieutenant was in love with her, and he had proposed to Amelia instead.

"I never realised your accommodation was so near Keighley before," a voice remarked at her shoulder.

Lilac, who had been gazing into a shop window, started violently. She swung round to face Chance Harland who stood but a pace behind her.

"Are you following me?" she began.

"Alas, sometimes I have other things to occupy my time," he said. "You handle the mare very well, by the by. I would have told you yesterday, but you made a somewhat precipitate departure."

"Which can easily be repeated, sir," she said, her eyes glinting.

"We were both a trifle hasty. I ought to have more tactfully phrased my request that you safeguard yourself by not riding too far afield. Am I forgiven?"

Now was the moment to inform him righteously that she objected to his trifling with one of the servants but that would be to admit she had spied on him. Instead, she heard herself say, "It is only that I dislike it when you treat me like a foolish child, Mr Harland. You are not so very elderly yourself, you know."

"Ouch." He gave her a startled look and then laughed, the harsh planes of his face becoming boyish and charming. "You may be small, Miss Lilac—may I call you so? Lilac is a pretty name."

"If you wish, Mr Harland," she said stiffly.

"My grandfather's name was Mr Harland," he said. "I cannot recall anybody calling him by his Christian name. If I am to retain my own identity and not begin to imagine myself as even older than I am, I would be grateful if you would use my first name too."

"Mr Chance then."

"I was saying, Miss Lilac, that you may be small, but you have a powerful punch. Are you a devotee of the noble sport of boxing? No, of course you are not. Your game is billiards, is it not? And what brings you into Keighley?"

"I wish to enquire at the parish church as to the whereabouts of my grandparents' graves. I felt that it would be a respectful gesture if I made certain that they are being looked after."

The smile died on his face. For an instant she fancied he was going to give her some sharp and sarcastic answer. Instead, after an almost imperceptible hesitation, he said,

"It seems that I have come to the rescue again. The Mortons were buried in Hull."

"In Hull? Who buried them in Hull?" she exclaimed.

"The undertaker, I assume," he said. "No, don't bridle at me. That was in the worst possible taste, and I apologize unreservedly. I understand that the family came originally from there. Consequently, they were buried there. I am sure their graves are well kept, so there is no need for you to gallop off in that direction."

"It would have been only a duty visit anyway," she confessed.

"How inconvenient it must be to have a conscience," he remarked. "I will admit to you though, Miss Lilac, that your arrival has stirred my own. I rode by Sladen Hall this morning and gave Fanny some money I'd owed her for months."

This was the last thing she had expected to hear. She stared at him for a moment.

"I had some guests a while back," he continued, "and could get no extra help. Fanny agreed to come over and assist for the evening, and I neglected to pay the poor girl. As it was, I had to throw stones at three windows before I hit on the right one and she bestirred herself."

"Why come by so early then?"

"I wanted to make an early start as I'd a couple of sheep

farms from which to collect the rents. My agent is on holiday, so I rode over myself."

Ridiculous or not, such a rush of relief flooded Lilac at his words that she turned a beaming face to him.

"Oh, if you wish to have a carouse you may borrow Fanny any time."

He was laughing again, the shadow vanished from his face. "Miss Lilac, you are an original," he said. "I have finished my day's business now. May I take you to dinner. In these savage parts dinner is eaten at midday and high tea in the evening, though I fear that London habits are infiltrating. Will you come? There is a most respectable inn to which not even the most puritanical could object."

"Do you really consider me to be puritanical?" she enquired anxiously.

"I consider you completely charming," he said and tucked her hand into his arm with an air that made her feel as if her broken heart were merely cracked after all.

The inn was all he had affirmed. The landlord looked as much like a bishop as is possible without actually wearing gaiters. The meal was heavier than she was used to in the middle of the day, but the ride had given her an appetite. She did full justice to the steak and kidney pie, the roasted parsnips and peas, the apple pie and cheese. Chance kept up a lively conversation throughout, as if he sought to make amends for his previous curtness. He had a fund of amusing stories about his boyhood, when he and Mark Sladen shared lessons and occasionally defied authority.

"We dressed up once as highwaymen and sought to increase our pocket money by relieving a few travellers of their possessions. I was eleven and Mark a couple of years older. It never entered our heads that we were both somewhat small and our voices decidedly high pitched for desperate robbers. We were recognised at once and hauled before our respective families."

"Were you severely punished?" Lilac asked.

"Mark was beaten, but my tender youth saved me. My

grandfather took me to York to show me what happened to those who took up robbery as a full time profession. It was the first time I'd ever seen a man hanged. I have seen such events since, but none has had so great an effect. I decided then that my choice of profession must lie elsewhere."

"I never saw an execution," Lilac said. "I don't believe that I would like it at all."

"It is not the hanging that is the worst," he told her. "It is the pleasure and excitement of the crowd. Human beings in the mass are not pretty."

"Alice and I thought you were a highwayman when you rode up to the coach on the night we arrived," she told him.

"And were ready to defend your possessions no doubt?"

"Also our honour."

"I am sorry to spoil your romantic illusions," he said, grinning, "but most thieves are too anxious to grab their loot and be away to have much thought of anything else."

"Well, we were vastly relieved that you were not a robber," she said, laughing.

"Only a rather churlish neighbour, I'm afraid. You will take a coffee?"

"It was an excellent meal."

"Yorkshire cooking is justly famous," he said. "I have eaten well in many places, but I still give my native county the prize."

"You make me more determined than ever to stay," Lilac said.

"A girl like yourself deserves a more brilliant setting than a neglected house in the middle of nowhere."

"You exaggerate the isolation," she protested. "I hope to spend a few days in York before the winter sets in. I shall take Alice with me and stay in a respectable hotel. There are functions one may attend even when one is not out."

"York!"

The smile had vanished from his face, and she could have sworn there was dismay in his exclamation. She told herself she must have been mistaken, for a moment later he was speaking in an easy tone once more.

"I'm told the society is very genteel in York. I seldom go there save now and then on business."

"If my grandmother had lived she would have provided me with the right introductions," Lilac said regretfully. "She was herself a deeply religious lady, though not, I fancy, as narrow as the Mortons seem to have been. She would have made sure I was properly launched."

"As you say." He sounded as if he were thinking of something else.

"I will meet more people when I attend Service, I daresay," Lilac continued. "I was going to enquire where you worshipped, sir."

"Not in any place where preachers tread," Chance said wryly. "I am not a lover of churches."

"You never go?" Lilac stared at him, never having talked with an infidel before. "Mr Chance, everybody goes somewhere. Even the Catholics go to their Mass."

"I choose not," he said, "but nobody ever bothers me about it. When one does not live in town one is not expected to conform rigidly."

"I shall certainly go to church," Lilac said firmly. "Which is the nearest?"

"Haworth, I suppose." He spoke with obvious reluctance. "Mr Charnock is by way of being an invalid so his sermons are, I'm told, mercifully short. I do not, however, avail myself of them."

"I shall," said Lilac.

"As you please. Will you take more coffee?"

"I am so full, that I am likely to burst," she said, "if you will pardon such an inelegant expression."

"Elegance in young girls is too artificial for my tastes and bores me." He shot her one of his quick, attractive smiles. "It is a long time since I have had the pleasure of enjoying the company of a pretty girl who is natural and does not spoil herself with posing and posturing."

"Yet you would still have me return south," she challenged.

"Miss Lilac, I confess to you freely that I am no longer so certain exactly what I would have." He sounded exasperated though he was still smiling.

"I know what you mean," she exclaimed, "for I have the same difficulty myself. Only a week or two ago I believed that I knew exactly what I wanted, and now I am no longer so sure . . . save that I would like to stay here in the north for the six months which I rented Sladen Hall. I might even choose to remain for a longer time."

"We will ride back." He had risen and his voice was abrupt once again. "I have completed my business and will see you safe home." The smile had fled from his face, but there was a tenderness lurking at the back of his eyes.

== 13 ==

RIDING HOME WITH him Lilac was conscious of pleasure in his company, though they spoke little. The day had remained fine, the sun a sheen of gold over the browning heather. The wind already held autumn in its breath, but the air was thick with bee humming.

"They feed on the heather," Chance explained. "Did you never taste heather honey fresh from the comb? Until you have, you cannot tell what perfect honey tastes like."

"Do bees feed on lilacs?"

"There's also lilac honey," he said, smiling slightly. "That flavour is more subtle."

"I intend to make the lilac garden beautiful again," she told him. "It was my mother's favourite flower, and just before she died she named me for it. I like to imagine that she saw the lilacs at Sladen Hall."

"As a matter of fact she did." Chance sounded as if he had remembered something. "In the spring—yes, it was spring because we'd been over to check on how the young lambs were doing—"

"We?"

"Mark and I. We had begun to fancy ourselves as landowners. Your mother was by the house when we rode down the bridle path. She had been walking on the moor and was thirsty. Mark invited her in but she refused. Afraid if the Mortons found out, I suppose. Anyway he brought her some water and she asked if he would object to her walking in the lilac garden for a while. Mark gave her leave and she went off."

"And that was all?" Lilac felt obscurely disappointed.

"I told you I hardly knew her. I was at an age when I admired young ladies with more obvious charms. I was on rather bad terms with her husband."

"He disapproved of you?"

"Only slightly less than his parents did." Chance grimaced.

"What did you do?" Lilac asked with interest. "Apart from dressing up as a highwayman, I mean."

"My grandfather had recently died. I sowed my wild oats with tremendous enthusiasm."

"Oh." Lilac blushed and remembered the orange dress.

"You are prettier than your mother was," he said abruptly. "You have more life in your face. She seemed cast down, depressed . . . not as a bride ought to be."

She had been afraid, Lilac thought. Of what?

They were nearing Sladen Hall, and she had a sense of homecoming.

"I hope you are demanding a reduction in your rent for all the work being put in here." Chance spoke in a practical tone as if to nullify the compliment he had just paid her.

"I am enjoying it," she protested. "I like to see the house begin to live again. I think it's a pity when a house dies after the people have left it."

"You may be right. Will you have dinner with me on Saturday evening?"

"Where?" she asked, feeling a sudden confusion at the invitation.

"In my house. You may bring Alice as chaperone, but she can eat with Nathan and John. They are in dire need of feminine conversation."

"If you truly wish me to come and are not just being polite," she said at last.

"Surely you've learned by now that I am seldom polite?" He shot her a glance that was pure mischief. "I will admit though that you are having an excellent influence over me. Soon I will be practising London manners. You will note I asked you for dinner?"

"In London they dine at eight."

"I will send Nathan over to collect you at six unless it rains, in which case, we will dine on Sunday at the same hour. Good day to you, Lilac Morton."

He was gone before she had time to ask him if he would take some refreshment.

"Go out to dinner?" Alice echoed when she was informed. "I'm sure I don't know. Me sitting with two strange men?"

"Nathan and John are very ordinary men," Lilac said amused. "If you require help you can call out to Mr Harland and myself."

"As long as it don't turn into an orgy," Alice said at last.

"With you half a glass of cooking sherry would constitute an orgy," Lilac said, laughing.

"Well, seeing as 'ow you said yes." Alice capitulated. "I must say that you look none the worse for riding all over the place. Got quite a colour in your cheeks."

It was true, Lilac thought, looking in her mirror later. Her city complexion was now rosy and her black hair had a sheen on it that was almost blue-black. She gave her reflection a little grimace. Amelia was married by now, and Lilac's own true love would never come again. Yet, she showed no trace of heartbreak in her features nor in the eager expression of her vivid eyes. It was, therefore, provoking in the extreme that on Saturday night the skies opened and the rain poured down.

Alice looked through the window and tried to hide her relief.

"It might not have bin an 'appy occasion, Miss Lilac," she said.

"We shall be going tomorrow if the weather improves," Lilac responded unfeeling. "So you had best resign yourself, and don't you dare pray for more wet weather."

"No, miss," Alice said, and sighed.

The evening seemed longer than usual. Lilac, who had previously been perfectly content to sit by the fire and read or chat with Alice, felt suddenly restless and deprived. It would have been stimulating to spend an evening at Harland House.

She had no idea what she felt about Chance because he never seemed to be in the same mood for more than a few minutes at a time. Yet she was bound to admit to herself that she was attracted to him. She wished she could decide in what the attraction lay since he was certainly not as handsome or charming as Peter Wentworth. Still, he had a smile that came so rarely and swiftly that she found herself waiting for it, and he was taller with hands that were a combination of gentleness and strength. Neither was he so old. When he was ninety she would be seventy, and they would match very well.

"Tomorrow we will go to church," she told Alice.

"There's no bottom to the carriage," Alice pointed out.

"You will ride Pegasus and I will ride Daisy; and don't tell me you've never been on a horse in all your born days, for riding Pegasus is the easiest thing in the world."

Alice cast her eyes up to heaven but said nothing. No doubt she was praying for a cloudburst, Lilac thought. Nonetheless, the next morning the rain had ceased save for a slight drizzle. Lilac had put on her habit and gone down into the yard when Alice, vainly trying to conceal her relief, came to tell her that there was only the one lady's saddle.

"Nonsense. Daisy was lent to me complete with saddle," Lilac said, "And there is the one Elijah found for Pegasus."

"Leather's cracked right across, Miss," Alice said. "I couldn't be expected to sit on it in that condition, now could I."

"No, of course not. I shall have to go alone then." Lilac was not too displeased. Alice would have grumbled terribly all the way.

"T'becks in flood again," Fanny announced, popping her head out of the kitchen door.

"Aye, that it is," Elijah agreed.

"Then I will skirt round the beck. Someone from this household must set an example."

Lilac mounted up, thinking that it was much more exciting to be riding to service over the moor than in a stuffy coach.

The beck was certainly in flood, pretending to be a river and making it necessary for her to take a wide detour. The long grasses held the rain, and she was glad that Daisy was surefooted as the horse picked her way unerringly between the patches of bog. Haworth lay to the northeast, past Stanmore. It was not a long way as the crow flies; but, not being a crow, Lilac was forced to abide by the rise and fall of the contours of the land.

A subtle and haunting land, she thought, and wished she was talented with oils or watercolours. In winter when the snows fell the landscape would cry out for charcoal, stark and dramatic, with a threatening aspect.

The gallop of hooves disturbed her musing; and she drew rein, expecting to spy a repentant Alice, but seeing instead the tall figure of Chance Harland as he caught up with her.

"Good morning, Miss Lilac." He doffed his hat politely. "I hope you were not too annoyed last night by the postponement of our engagement. I believe it will be possible tonight."

"I spent an exceedingly tedious evening," she said.

"I will endeavour to make up for it tonight. Nathan and John are looking forward to entertaining Alice while you and I sit sedately enjoying a sophisticated dinner."

"You are making fun of me," she accused. "That is not kind of you when I have my mind fixed on going to church."

"One must be gloomy for that? I had forgotten. It is a long time since I went."

"You should go more often," she said.

"Which is why I have been vainly trying to catch you up for the last five minutes."

"You are going to church?" she said in astonishment.

"You see what a salutary influence you are on me?" His eyes were twinkling. "You and I will now astonish the neighbours by walking in together as if we were the oldest of friends."

"I hope that we shall be," Lilac said impulsively. "Friends, I mean."

"Do you, Miss Lilac?" His gaze, lingering on her, made her spur Daisy ahead in a manner that would account for the warm colour in her cheeks.

The church was a barn-like narrow-windowed structure which stood at the top of the steep, cobbled street. As they dismounted and tethered their horses Lilac was conscious of curious glances from the people coming up the hill: plainly clad folk with shawls over their heads and thick soled clogs.

"It is not often," Chance murmured, offering his arm, "that a vision of beauty comes this way. Also they are now fearing that the end of the world is at hand since only the oldest can recall my coming to service."

"Oh, do hush," Lilac begged, stifling a giggle as Chance swept off his hat to announce loudly, "A prayerful morning, Mrs Ackroyd. Do you not agree?"

The woman thus addressed was in her early thirties, neatly dressed, with bonnet instead of shawl.

"It's that right enough, sir," she agreed. "Coming in, are you?"

"Naturally." Chance held open the door with an air of innocence that made Lilac want to giggle once again.

Inside there were high pews and a row of benches upon which children were already fidgeting.

"The Harland pew," Chance whispered. He opened the half door and escorted her in with something of a flourish.

The service was long mainly because the Reverend Mr

Charnock spoke very slowly. He looked pale and tired. Lilac guessed that he too would have liked to cut everything short but lacked the necessary energy. As the sermon meandered, she was increasingly conscious of the proximity of Chance Harland's tall, well-built figure.

The singing was lusty, the congregation clearly enjoying itself. Lilac, whose own voice never managed to hold the key, hummed discreetly while Chance raised a pleasant tenor. The service over they came out into the sunshine again. It had been chilly inside, and Lilac lifted her face to the blue sky.

"Ought we not to wait to greet the minister?" she objected as her companion took her arm to help her mount.

"Listening to Mr Charnock is sufficient evil unto the day," Chance said. "I do not propose to have a long conversation with him as well. He will be as anxious for his dinner as we are, make no mistake."

The children were clattering out, obviously delighted to be set free. Lilac smiled in sympathy, remembering long hours she had spent with her grandmother frowning every time she shuffled her feet. One or two of the bigger children had paused to stare curiously before running on.

"I hoped to meet some of the neighbours," she began.

"You are accustomed to churches in London," Chance said. "There one goes to see and be seen. Here people are more insular. You would have to live among them for ten years before they gave you the time of day."

They might not be talking to her, she thought, though one or two had nodded; but they certainly seemed to be talking about her. Little knots were gathering and glancing in her direction. She wondered what they were saying. Perhaps some of them remembered her mother. She wished that she were alone so she could get down and introduce herself, but Chance had mounted up himself and taken Daisy's leading rein. Clearly he had no desire to fraternise with the rest of the congregation. When the woman he had addressed as Mrs Ackroyd took a step towards them, he jerked on Daisy's rein to pull her into a trot.

"You must be in a great hurry for your food," Lilac said sharply, grabbing the rein back.

"Sermons make me irritable," was all he said, and indeed his earlier affability had fled.

They rode home in silence: Chance apparently intent on avoiding the pitfalls in the flooded grass, Lilac deciding crossly that the next time she came to church she would come alone and try to make contact with her neighbours.

"I will send Nathan at six," he said as they neared the beck. "I doubt if it will rain again tonight, but wrap up warmly. The wind can be treacherous."

"Alice will require a saddle," she remembered. "The only other lady's saddle is not fit."

"I'll send an extra one." He drew rein suddenly, looking at her with a quizzical expression. "Have you got the churchgoing out of your system?"

"Until next week," she said obstinately.

"A lot can happen in a week," he said and set his horse at a gallop with no more than a brief wave of his crop.

Staring after him, Lilac was filled with contradictory emotions. It had been good of him to escort her, but he had hurried her away so fast she was bewildered. As she rode more sedately through the gates of Sladen Hall, it occurred to her he hadn't wanted her to talk to anybody. She wondered what possible reason he could have for that.

= 14 =

IT WAS TOO cold to wear the flimsy chiffon dress which was the prettiest she had brought with her. Since she was riding to Harland House, it would be sensible to wear a habit anyway; but one could scarcely have dinner in a riding habit. Lilac dragged every garment out of the wardrobe before reminding herself that Chance probably wouldn't notice what she had on anyway. A man who made love to girls in bright orange was not a man well versed in the niceties of feminine apparel. Lilac had a new habit of dove grey with a basque jacket trimmed with scarlet, and that would do very well.

Having decided that, she spent another couple of hours experimenting with her hair. Barbara had always set her face against cutting or frizzing it up into curls, but Lilac looked impossibly young with it hanging in a tail down her back. In the end she got Alice to pin it into a heavy knot that tilted her head back and showed her long slim neck.

Lilac was ready before six, a circumstance that irritated her since she had no wish to appear too eager. Nathan duly put in an appearance, bringing an extra saddle for Alice who, despite her avowed disinclination to go, had donned her best skirt and a bonnet with two roses coyly tucked under the brim.

It was a magnificent evening. The far distant hills shaded into mauve and purple, and the nearer landscape was tinted pink and rust by the fast-falling sun. Above the riders, the sky shone dappled blue which turned to silver-grey as shadows lengthened.

"Weel, 'e's got a nice 'ouse," Alice admitted in an undertone as they turned in at the gate.

Lilac agreed, smiling as she nodded.

The building had a weathered aspect that blended well with the ivied walls. The house was smaller than Sladen Hall and lacked the open views that surrounded Morton Grange, but it was a house in which one might live very comfortably. Lilac banished such musings and allowed Nathan to help her down from the saddle. John opened the front door with an air of grave and respectful formality. He was looking considerably neater than the last time she had seen him.

"If you would come this way, Miss Morton?"

"This way" led down the corridor into a long room where masculine severity had been tempered by gracefully draped curtains and a copper bowl filled with autumn flowers. Chance came forward to greet her; and, looking at him, Lilac regretted the chiffon gown. This evening he was almost handsome and certainly distinguished in light grey breeches and frilled evening shirt under a tight jacket, his cravat elaborately tied, his shoes brilliant.

"Good evening, Alice. If you will go with John there is a repast waiting for you," Chance said, giving Alice a smile that melted any objection she might have been entertaining.

"Delighted, I'm sure, sir," Alice said. The glance she shot Lilac said plainly, "All that worry, and him a perfect gentleman."

"Nathan is going to change and then serve our meal," said Chance as Alice went out with John.

"I'm sure it will be an excellent one," Lilac said.

"Are you intending to remove your hat?" he enquired. "It is some considerable time since I was in the south, and I'm not certain if ladies now wear their hats indoors or not."

Lilac took one look at his twitching mouth and found herself laughing.

"All this formality is to tease me, I see," she exclaimed.

"I don't want you to return to London and tell your friends we are all complete savages here."

"I do wish that the moment you lay eyes on me you thought of something other than my departure," she retorted.

"You are set upon remaining? Quite set?"

"Absolutely. The more you inform me of the disadvantages of the country, the more I am enamoured of it."

"Then let us drink to your time here. You do take sherry wine?"

"Yes, of course." She accepted the glass and the chair he indicated, then looked up at him questioningly.

"Why did you attend the service this morning and then hurry me away so rapidly? Pray don't try to make me believe that you had a sudden conversion."

"It was a whim on my part." He shrugged.

"And one quickly regretted, I suspect?"

"I did warn you that I am not one for the conventions."

"Then you need not have come," she said. "I do hope that you are not beginning to regard me in the light of a responsibility. I am well able to take care of myself."

"I will grant that you have a sense of adventure," he said. "To rush up to a strange part of the country with the object of spending six months in a house you haven't even seen is not the action of a stay-at-home. But you are still only seventeen."

"Eighteen in January." She lifted her chin.

"And in need of a protector."

"Mr Harland." Lilac's cheeks crimsoned as she stared at him. "I may be here without a real chaperone, but that does not give you the right to ask me to be your—your mistress."

"Mistress? I want you as my wife," he shot back.

They went on staring at each other for a moment. Then Chance gave a short, rueful laugh.

"I had everything planned," he said. "Over the soup I was going to give you details of my illustrious ancestry. Then during the fish you would have been regaled with my educational record. Upon the serving of the main course I would have endeavoured to convey my feelings of respect and affection. By the time we reached dessert the ground would have been prepared for a formal proposal. But instead, I blurt it out like an untried schoolboy."

"Your wife?" Lilac repeated. Her face had paled.

"You are going to tell me it is out of the question," he said. "I am twenty years older than you and have been boasting since we met of my ramshackle life. You have come for six months only, after which you will return to London and marry some gallant, young officer who missed the last boat to India. Of course, it is quite impossible that you should dream of—"

"I accept," said Lilac and closed her mouth on the phrase as if it had escaped her unaware.

"You accept?" Chance stood, gazing not at her but at the dregs in his glass.

"I—I misunderstood you at first," she said, stammering slightly in her confusion. "You have painted yourself in rather a bad light, you know. You really cannot blame me for leaping to the wrong conclusion. If it is a wife you are seeking then I shall be very happy to accept."

"Splendid." He drained his glass.

Lilac had the feeling that he was as nervous as she. "Was that why you were so out of temper this morning?" she enquired. "You were still trying to decide whether or not to ask me."

"Oh, I decided to ask you when you made it clear that all my discouraging words were not going to chase you away," he said. "I have been arguing with myself about it for several days. Many people would advise a longer acquaintanceship, a protracted engagement; but I have always been of the opinion that if you decide to do something it is best to do it at once."

"Oh, so have I," Lilac exclaimed fervently.

"You will require your uncle's consent, of course. Do you have his address?"

"Only his last known one. I don't know if he is informed of my grandmother's death yet."

"There is a family lawyer, I presume? He might be in a position of *in loco parentis*. Do you have his address?"

"Yes, of course," Lilac felt slightly bewildered. "You are very businesslike, aren't you?"

"I am hoping to gain permission from whomever is your legal guardian as soon as possible," he told her. "I have never proposed marriage to anybody before; but, having taken the first plunge, I intend to swim into deep water. Perhaps I am afraid you may change your mind."

"Indeed I won't," she protested. "I must tell you that I am not rich. There was an entail on the property, and everything belongs to Uncle Philip."

"I was not thinking of marrying you for your money," he said with a slight smile. "I am not a man of tremendous wealth myself. However, I can certainly support you comfortably; and, as I have no relatives living, what I possess will be yours when I am gone."

"You are the most extraordinary man I ever met," Lilac said. "You propose marriage and at once begin discussing your funeral."

"I wished you to be sure that you will be safe, financially secure. If you crave loverlike talk I fear you'll be disappointed, for I was never a demonstrative man. In Yorkshire we are not."

"I can see that," Lilac said.

Chance laughed suddenly, then took the glass from her hand and drew her to her feet. She was conscious once more of his scent of bay and lemon and masculinity.

"But we do know how to kiss up in Yorkshire," he said and bent his head, his lips warm and seeking.

Lilac had imagined being kissed by a boy, but this was a man and an experienced one. She told herself that he would likely be disappointed by her own inexperience, and then she didn't think about anything at all for several minutes.

"You're very charming, Lilac Mary Morton."

As she opened her eyes he was stepping back a pace, his hands still on her shoulders, his voice gentle.

"Thank you, sir. Chance?" She gave him a mischievous look.

"Chance most certainly," he agreed promptly. "I am not of the school of thought that considers one must be married and six months pass before one uses first names."

"Nor that one should starve to death while one is talking about marriage?"

"Dinner." He gave her a rueful look. "I can tell you will be an excellent wife for you will remind me of important things like eating at the right times and not coming in with muddy boots."

"And now you may enjoy your dinner," she said, "without the necessity of working up to a proposal."

"Come. Nathan will be entertaining Alice and forgetting his duties." He offered his arm, and they went through to the dining room which was elegantly laid with silver and crystal. Perhaps he had spoken the truth when he said he was apprehensive.

"You were going to tell me about your illustrious ancestors," she invited when they were seated and the soup had been served.

"Indeed I was." He smiled at her. "The Harlands settled Yorkshire in the Viking age, and the red hair that crops up in every other generation is a legacy of Harold the Red who ate his meat raw because he could never find a cook to suit him. Will you marry me soon, the moment I receive the requisite permission?"

"Spring is a pleasant time for weddings," she began.

"If permission can be obtained before then, I see no reason for delay," Chance said. "I will write to your family lawyer, explaining that we are anxious to be married before Advent. Then you can go down to London and begin making the arrangements. I assume you will want to be married from your grandmother's—that is, your uncle's house?"

"I suppose so," she said blankly. It was odd, but she had never actually considered the practical details of a wedding before. She and Amelia had discussed endlessly the dresses they planned to wear and the flowers they would carry. That banns must be called and licences bought had seemed unimportant.

"I would suggest your leaving in about a week," Chance Harland said. "I will settle things here, and then join you with the licence in my pocket. What is it?"

Trout was being served and the soup plates removed. Lilac hesitated until they were alone gain.

"It all seems rushed, somehow. I accepted an invitation to dinner, and now we are calling the banns."

"Winter in any part of England is dreary," Chance said easily. "I hoped to spend the winter abroad. You would enjoy Italy, I think. I have not been there since my grandfather sent me on the Grand Tour."

"To winter in Italy? Oh, I would like it above all things." Lilac clasped her hands together, her eyes shining.

"Then it must be soon. I doubt if your guardian would approve of your running off to Italy with me without a wedding ring on your finger."

"I suppose not." Lilac wondered fleetingly if Uncle Philip would much care. He had never taken the least interest in her.

"It is agreed then?"

He was smiling at her, but there was something at the back of his eyes that was not joyful.

"Yes, it's agreed," she said.

Chance pushed back his chair and rose. "I have a gift for you. I hoped I would have the right to give it to you before the evening was over." He went to a cupboard in the wall by the high mantel shelf. "It belonged to my mother who was happy with my father and was given to me for the woman I wished to make happy," he said. "I am anxious to make you happy, Lilac."

It was a ring, diamonds sparkling round a saphhire.

"My mother also had blue eyes," he said softly. "Not as vivid as yours but a pretty shade. She would have approved of you, I think."

"It is lovely. A fraction too large, I think?"

"It can be secured with thread. I'll come by in a couple of days and take it to be made smaller." He put his hand over hers briefly and warmly, and the shadow was gone.

"When did you decide to—to propose?" Lilac asked shyly. "I mean—you only asked me to dinner last night? You could not have had it in your mind for long."

"Why not?" He was eating his meal as if there was nothing more romantic on his mind that roast veal.

"You teased me from the first moment," she accused. "You were forever pointing out your great age, and telling me to go home, and making it plain that you considered me a ninny."

"I suppose I was seeking to convince myself," he said. "I have lived as a happy bachelor for a long time, which is not to say I was never in love. I fell in and out of love with the seasons, and forgot their faces when a new season was come. The moment you came dripping into my house I knew that I would not easily forget your face; and, within a short space of time, I didn't want to forget."

"I would like to know one thing," she said, "though I've no doubt it is very shocking of me."

"What do you want to know?" His tone was indulgent.

"Who owned the orange dress," she said. "I could not believe that any lady would choose such a colour."

"You are correct. No lady would. Maude was not, however, from the upper classes of society though she would have been most offended had you told her that. She came for three months and flounced out after three weeks declaring she was sick and tired of the country and of me. By then the feeling was mutual, I promise you."

"I should not have asked."

"You should not," he agreed amiably. "Now, if it is to be confession time, are there any orange dresses in your life?"

"I have many friends," she said.

"But no lovers—unless you started in your cradle?"

She had thought she loved Lieutenant Peter Wentworth and fancied he had loved her. The latter hadn't been true, so perhaps the former wasn't either.

"No lovers," she said and drank her wine.

"And you are happy to be engaged? No second thoughts?"

He spoke lightly, but the shadow was back in his eyes.

"None at all," she said, and hoped it was true.

Everything was happening so quickly that she felt as if she were on a long slide that had begun to take her away from everything familiar. In a little while she would know how she felt about things, but at this moment she could only wonder vaguely what on earth she was doing eating her dinner with a ring on her finger that was too big and a man she hardly knew.

= 15 =

"You could 'ave knocked me down with a feather, miss,"
Alice said dramatically. "Just hearing you say that you
intend getting wed to Mr Harland, and I come over queer."

"It surprised me too," Lilac admitted.

"Well, when you meet Mr Right there's no argument
against Fate," Alice said wisely.

"No, I suppose not," Lilac spoke thoughtfully, but her
face was serious and troubled. Anybody guessing the trend
of her thoughts at that moment would not have picked
marriage as the subject of them.

Actually, she wasn't in the least certain she was doing
the right thing. Falling in love ought to be similar on each
occasion, but her feelings for Chance Harland bore no
resemblance to the emotions that filled her when she
thought of Peter Wentworth. The latter had made her feel
breathless and gay, but Chance frequently puzzled and
irritated her. She was not sure if it was love she felt for him
at all, and she was not sure if the feeling he had for her was
love either.

Lilac gave a sigh, wishing she could make these things
clear in her own mind. The proposal had come so unexpectedly, and she had accepted with the same speed. Now,
sitting by the fire in Sladen Hall, she began to fear she
might be one of those women who, disappointed in one
direction, leap in another merely for the sake of catching a
husband.

"I will communicate with your lawyer at once," he had

said briskly, taking down the address. "Even if your uncle cannot be contacted I forsee no great difficulty. You will return to London next week and have the banns posted in your local church while I obtain a licence."

He had been as businesslike as if he were accustomed to getting married every day. Even his kiss before he went to call Nathan to ride back with her and Alice had been perfunctory. She reminded herself that his earlier kiss had been warm and exciting. No doubt he had the practical details on his mind, but she would have appreciated a little more romance.

It was all happening too quickly. She had come up into Yorkshire to find out about her mother, and she had found out nothing worth hearing. Her grandparents were dead and seemed to have been unpleasant people, and there the trail had come to a dead end, leaving her with a curious feeling of dissatisfaction.

Yet, she couldn't avoid the way her heart leapt when she looked out of the window the next morning and saw Chance riding up to the door. He sat his horse well, she told herself; and, even if he was not conventionally handsome, he had a charming smile. Furthermore, his reputation as a rake, about which he seemed quite amused, was probably exaggerated.

"I came to collect the ring," he told her when she went down to greet him.

For an instant she imagined that he had changed his mind and was going to tell her it had all been a mistake and he didn't want to marry her at all. Then she recalled that the ring needed altering.

"Yes, of course." She took it from her finger and gave it to him.

"It will be ready in a few days. I'll reserve your seats on the stage while I'm in Keighley. Is something wrong?"

"I shall miss the ring," she said, smiling. At the back of her head a voice was insisting, "He wanted you to leave, and now you are leaving."

"When I woke up this morning," he said, taking her hand as they walked into the parlour, "I found it difficult to believe that I'd actually proposed marriage."

"I found it difficult to believe that I'd actually accepted," she rejoined.

"I hope you're not regretting it? You seem . . . " He looked down at her, searching for words.

"Bewildered," she supplied. "I never expected to be an engaged lady after dinner last night."

"I want you to be happy with me," he said. "I want to make you happy. I am very sure that this is the right thing to do."

The bronze eyes were warm and kind, but the protection he offered was motivated by something other than loving. Lilac could feel that through to her bones and hoped the knowledge didn't show in her face. Chance, in the meantime, continued the conversation as if he noticed nothing.

"If you like, I'll contact this young man who inherited the house and offer to oversee its renovation. I suspect that you don't want to leave something half-finished."

"If it was in really good condition he could rent it out," she agreed, "and obtain a better price for it."

"We may turn you into a business woman yet," he said lightly and kissed her cheek.

"I do want to be married," she said impulsively. "Truly I do."

"So do I." He cocked an eyebrow at her and flashed the smile that made him look so much younger.

"And Italy will be perfect for a honeymoon. The Italians have a treat in store."

Chance moved away a few steps and looked around the room. "I never came in here when I was a boy," he said. "Mrs Sladen used to sit here and sew. It was her retreat from two rather noisy little boys. She was a pleasant lady and this was a happy house. I realise now, that in letting me come here during the week, my grandfather was giving me a taste of family life."

"Your own parents died?"

If she could build up a picture of his life then she would be able to understand him better, perhaps even understand why he had so suddenly proposed.

"Carriage accident," he said briefly.

"And the Sladens?"

"Mr Sladen died of a heart attack while Mark and I were still schoolboys, and Mrs Sladen of the influenza later on. Isn't this conversation becoming rather gloomy?"

"I was merely interested in learning about past neighbours."

"The future is what's important," Chance said. "I feel it a mistake to live too much in the past. We cannot alter any of it. so why not look ahead?"

"I suppose you are right," she agreed. "At least my own life has been remarkably dull until now."

"No passionate love affairs?"

He spoke lightly, but she blushed all the same.

"I said dull," she countered.

"From one or two remarks you let fall, I imagined that you might have had a *tendresse* for some young man."

He was too shrewd. Lilac blushed more deeply, then raised her eyes to his.

"There was a young man," she said honestly. "I scarcely knew him, but I fancied he admired me. I was obviously mistaken for he proposed to my best friend, and now I see that he was just flirting with me while he made up his mind to wed Amelia. My pride was hurt, but it was only pride."

"I'm glad." Chance put his arm about her waist and kissed her cheek again. "I warn you that I am of a somewhat jealous temperament and will countenance no lieutenants—I assume he was such—hanging about my door and ogling my bride."

"He went to India and Amelia is to follow," Lilac said. The words had a wistful cadence.

"Splendid," Chance said. "I wish them happiness. Now

I had best make a start, for I've other business to attend as well as the ring. What will you do with yourself today?"

"This may astonish you," she said, "but long before I met you I was able to occupy my time profitably without having to be constantly amused."

"An independent lady. Splendid." He smiled at her as he moved away. "I will probably call the day after tomorrow, since tomorrow I must attend a sale of sheep. Occupy yourself profitably until then."

He was laughing as he went down the steps, and she smiled after him, the wistfulness fading. Chance Harland had a sense of humour that matched with her own, and he became more attractive the longer she knew him. She was beginning to be more certain of her decision.

She was still determined, however, to find out more about her family. Chance had said the past was not important. However, to her way of thinking, it shaped the future; and that made it more important than he was willing to admit. Lilac marched resolutely out to the yard and instructed Elijah to saddle Daisy. Alice was occupied in the linen closets. Thus, Lilac was able to ride out without having to offer a long string of explanations.

It was definitely colder this morning. She could feel the nip in the air and see the first sparkle of frost on the grass. The heather was browning, and a clump of harebells hung whitening heads. By the time the snows came, she and Chance would be in Italy, and she would know what it was like to be a married lady. The prospect of that brought colour to her face again. There was no lady to advise her as to what she should expect. She decided she might have a word with Alice, who though herself unmarried, was likely able to supply details.

Sheep grazed near Morton Grange this morning. Lilac dismounted and to walk over the grass. Even in sunlight the farmhouse had a deserted air. She tried to imagine how her mother must have felt as she walked out on the moor. Had she made plans for her coming child? Had she tried to work out in her own mind what was frightening her and longed for the necessary permission that would enable her and her husband to sail as missionaries to a new land?

The bishop. Lilac stopped short. Of course. There would be lists of missionaries and details of their careers kept in the church records. Those records would be at Wakefield or York, she supposed. She was foolish not to have thought of it before.

The sheep had a shepherd: a youngish man who ambled towards her now, his dog frisking ahead. She waited for him to draw level, and then saluted him politely.

"Good morning. Isn't it a fine day."

"It's a grand day," he returned. "Good to be out in't sun, miss."

"I was looking at the house." Lilac indicated the walls with their padlocked gate.

"The murder house," he nodded. "Aye, folks still come up from time to time t'tak a look."

"I beg your pardon?" Lilac stared at him, wondering if she had heard aright. "I fancied you to say the murder house? Surely it is Morton Grange?"

"Aye," he rejoined. "That's Morton Grange right enow, where t'murder took place. Eighteen years back, and the house empty since."

"There was a murder there?" Her voice had risen slightly.

"Unnatural and bloody," he said with a certain relish creeping into his tone.

"Who?" Her voice was hushed now, her eyes large.

"Man called Robert Morton killed his parents," the shepherd said.

The moor spun crazily around her. Lilac closed her eyes briefly, fighting for balance. It was not possible, she told herself. Her father had been killed by savages to whom he was taking the Gospel. He and her mother had sailed to America, and her mother returned alone to bear her child and die.

"Tha'd best sit down." The concerned voice of the shepherd jerked her back to reality. She opened her eyes and stared at him, the dizziness receding.

"I am perfectly well," she said. "I rode out without breakfast, that's all. You say a murder was committed here? How extremely unpleasant."

" 'Twas an unpleasant murder," he returned. "Shot them both he did. First the father and then the mother. Hanged for it at York."

Hearing the words spoken made it real. Despite the sunlight, the moor had become suddenly a dark place.

"Was . . . was he married?" she stirred herself to ask.

"Aye. I did hear as there was a wife. Never knew what happened to her though. Perhaps she died later on."

"Yes."

"If tha's thinking of renting," he said helpfully, "the property can likely be got cheap. Folk don't come here. There's a man caretakes, but he won't stay after dark."

"No, I wasn't thinking of renting," Lilac said. "I was merely curious who might live there."

"Nobody with any sense," he remarked.

"Nobody with any sense," she echoed. "No doubt you're right. Well, I must get on. Good-day to you."

She didn't hear his reply. Her one, overriding urge was to get away from there. She needed time for the information to sink in, time for the first shock to fade. She set Daisy at a canter, willing the past to recede as swiftly as the house was doing.

When she reached the grounds of Sladen Hall, she slowed to a walk, her head drooping. At that moment she wanted nothing more than to burst into tears, but that would be childish and stupid. She was obliged to find out the whole story now. It was possible there had been some mistake. Yet, she knew that wasn't true. There was no mistake. Robert Morton had killed his own parents and been hanged for it. He had never sailed to America at all. Grandmother had lied about everything.

That was in some way, the worst part of it all. Barbara had seemed so correct, so moral, and all the while she had been lying. Lilac wondered if any of their neighbours had known but thought it unlikely. Morton was not an uncommon name, and eighteen years ago a Yorkshire murder was not likely to have been much reported in London.

The minister at Haworth would surely have more accurate information. Lilac turned her mount in the direction of the village and was cantering off again almost before the decision had shaped itself in her mind. There might have been extenuating circumstances, some explanation why Robert Morton had been driven to do such a terrible deed.

The clacking of handlooms fell upon her ear as she rode down the narrow lane that led past the parsonage. A side gate opened onto a strip of garden. Lilac dismounted and secured Daisy's reins to a hook in the wall. Just then a woman came out of the house and gave her an enquiring look.

"T'Parson's over t'Stanmore this morning, miss," she said.

"Do you know when he will be back?" Lilac asked.

"He generally stops for a bite then rides on to Wycoller. Was it urgent?"

After eighteen years of deceit?

"No, not urgent," she said dully.

"Tha looks flushed," the woman said, her tone kindly "I could get thee a cup of water from t'well. I go in' parsonage to clean a bit on Mondays so it'd be no trouble

"Thank you, no. I don't require anything. Were you nc in church yesterday?" Lilac looked at her more closely

"I'm in church every Sunday," the woman said.

"Mrs Ackroyd? Am I correct?"

"Aye, and you'll be Miss Morton. The word's out that you came, though there's many still saying as tha died as a bairn."

"Everybody knows everything round here, it seems," Lilac said wryly.

"Nay, miss. There's them 'as knows and them 'as guesses," Mrs Ackroyd said scornfully. "Most folks reckon as it's thy business."

"I came to make enquiries about my . . . about the murder," Lilac said. "I don't know anything, you see."

"There's nowt left to tell," Mrs Ackroyd said discouragingly. "It were all thrashed out at the time."

"It's important for me to know why. Robert Morton shot both his parents. There had to be a good reason."

"There's never a good reason for shooting anybody," the other retorted, "but it were reckoned at the time he'd sufficient reason. They were hard, cold people, the Mortons. Like ice."

"And Robert, their son, did you know him?"

"Your father?" Mrs Ackroyd gave her a steady look.

"I was led to believe that he was going to be a missionary," Lilac said.

"There were talk of that," the other nodded. "He was brought to believe that the Lord were speaking to him, advising him in a personal way. He wanted to convert the heathen, but the bishop refused to recommend the appointment. Reckoned he were too fanatic."

"So he never went."

"In my opinion," Mrs Ackroyd said, "the dead ought to stay dead. No sense in muckraking."

"I have the right to know," Lilac said obstinately.

"Reckon so." Mrs Ackroyd hesitated, then took the younger woman by the arm. "Word came that Mary Morton and her baby had died," she said. "When we saw you in church we guessed the truth of it. There would have been some to question thee, but Mr Harland was with thee. So nowt was said for he's a powerful temper when it's roused, and it were plain he were protecting thee. The Mortons are laid in the graveyard here if tha wishes to see."

Lilac didn't wish to see, but she found herself accompanying the woman into the enormous and crowded churchyard. All around them, in every direction, headstones reared.

"They were set apart from the rest," Mrs Ackroyd said. "Not popular in life, nor in death; but that's not to say folks were glad to have them murdered."

The headstone bore only the two names and the dates, as if the history of those who lay beneath it was too well known to need repeating.

"Elias Morton, Born 1736 and Hannah Morton, née Fox, born 1740
　　Died 1799."

"In which month?" Lilac asked numbly.

"October," Mrs Ackroyd said. "Middle of October."

"I see." She spoke at random, looking at the bleak stone.

They had died just after her mother had penned the desperate little letter to Barbara, telling her she was afraid.

"It does no good to dig up the past," her companion said, her tone admonishingly kind. "Let the dead stay dead. Tha should not have come, lass."

"My mother, Mary Morton? Was she . . . did you know her?"

"Not really to speak," Mrs Ackroyd regretted. "I saw her at church on Sundays. Very bonny, she was with eyes like yourn, but sadder and paler. She used t' walk on't moor, they say. Walk for hours, aimless like as if she were trying to keep out of t'road. Not happy, for all she were carrying a babby. After the murder she went south, and then word came she'd died. Shows tha cannot trust rumour."

"She was here when it happened then?" Lilac felt a little thrill of horror.

"Robert Morton had just been turned down by t'church board again," Mrs Ackroyd told her. "He rode home and shot his parents, and then gave himself up. Mrs Mary were out for a walk else he might have killed her too. His lawyer tried to make out he were insane, but he were hanged anyway."

He must have been insane, Lilac thought. Driven mad by overzealous parents, and by his own frustration. And my mother felt the madness creeping up on him and was afraid.

"Tha really did not know?" Mrs Ackroyd was looking at her. "We took it that Mr Harland would have told thee, and not want us t' clack about it."

"He said nothing," Lilac said.

Instead he had tried to dissuade her from staying in the district and when that failed he'd hit upon an excuse to force her to go south again. No doubt once she was safely away from Yorkshire he would call off the wedding, rightly guessing that pride would hinder her from coming north again. Fanny and Elijah must know about it, and that was why he'd given Fanny money—to stop her tongue. It had nothing to do with back wages for any help she'd given him at a party.

"Are thee and Mr Harland thinking of getting wed?" Mrs Ackroyd asked.

"What?" Lilac stared at her blankly for a moment and then shook her head. "No," she said, and then again, "no."

= 16 =

LILAC'S FIRST INSTINCT was to flee back to London and never have to face Chance Harland again. However, a little reflection as she rode home convinced her of the folly of such a course. He had cared sufficiently about her peace of mind to deceive her. She had a shrewd suspicion that, if she were to tell him what she had discovered, he would beat down her objections and insist on going through with the ceremony. She would have to find some other reason for refusing him.

As she neared Sladen Hall, she thought suddenly that it was a good thing Peter Wentworth hadn't offered for her after all. He would not have been very pleased to find himself engaged to the daughter of a murderer. Unless he had offered and her grandmother told him the truth. Such a course of action would have been typical of her, since she would have regarded it her duty to warn any prospective suitor of the family history.

The longer Lilac pondered the more convinced she became that was exactly what had happened. He had made it so clear that he intended to ask her, and then he had suddenly proposed to Amelia instead. No man wanting to make his way in the world would relish the thought of a bride whose father had been hanged. Now she would probably never marry at all, as she too would feel obliged to tell any prospective husband the truth. Lilac wiped a stray tear from her cheek at the dismal thoughts crowding her head.

Fanny was in the stable yard, shaking crumbs from a tablecloth when Lilac rode in. She dismounted and went directly to her, asking without any preamble, "How much did Mr Harland pay you not to tell me about my father?"

"Five guin—" Fanny clapped her hand over her mouth and looked miserable.

"Does Alice know?"

"Oh, no, miss," Fanny assured her, crimson faced. "Mr Harland were most particular that thee both wasn't to be told. Elijah and me—we worred t'first evening, not sure who you were, but Mr Harland said not t'clack."

"Hold your tongue still, will you?" Lilac said. "I will tell Alice myself."

Lilac ran her maid to earth in the linen closet, sorting sheets, her brow furrowed. "I swear I darned this lot yesterday," she fretted. "They makes 'oles when me back is turned."

"Leave them be for now. I wish to talk to you." Lilac went into her bedroom, with Alice at her heels.

"Is something wrong, Miss Lilac? You're ever so pale." Alice looked apprehensive herself.

"Alice, I found out something extremely shocking this morning," Lilac began, sitting down on the bed.

"If it's about me and Elijah, miss—"

"No, it isn't about tha—what about you and Elijah?"

" 'Im and me," said Alice coyly, "are 'itting it off, in a manner of speaking."

"You mean he has made an offer for you?" Lilac looked at her in astonishment, momentarily diverted from her own troubles by the vision of the dour Elijah as a lover.

"Not yet, miss," Alice said, "but things are tending that way."

"I thought you hated Yorkshire."

"I'm getting used to it," Alice said placidly. "When 'e does offer I'm minded to say that I will."

"But we are going down to London next week," Lilac reminded her.

"That's only till the wedding, ain't it?" Alice said. "You and Mr Harland will be coming back 'ere afterwards to live."

Lilac's carefully prepared speech had fled. It would be unkind to confide in Alice now, to tell her the marriage proposal had been a ploy to get Lilac to leave the district so that she would suffer only the lesser hurt of a broken engagement instead of the shock of finding out she was the child of a man hanged for murder. Alice would come with her of course if she knew that, and miss her own chance of happiness.

"What was you wanting to say?" Alice enquired.

"Oh, about the gardens," Lilac answered vaguely. "I was thinking that it would be nice to begin to clear them ready for the spring."

"You're never expecting me to turn gardener, miss?" Alice said in horror. "I'll turn me 'and to any dirty job, but grub up worms I draw the line."

"No, of course I don't expect you to do it," Lilac said impatiently. "I wanted your opinion."

"My hopinion is that with all the improvements you're setting in hand, the owner of this place ought to pay you for staying 'ere," Alice said.

"Yes, well . . . Alice, I think it would be an excellent idea if you were to stay on here for a while," Lilac said in a distracted fashion. "I wouldn't wish your own plans to be spoilt by my returning south. As you say, we will be coming back—"

"And miss your wedding day? Why, Miss Lilac, I'd not dream of it," Alice exclaimed. "If Elijah fancies me, he won't stop just because I go to London for a few weeks. Might bring 'im to the point of asking me proper."

"I only thought—"

"And you could not go all the way by yourself," Alice continued firmly. "Why, Mrs Lameter would spin in her grave."

"You'd better finish sorting the linen," Lilac said in resignation.

"Yes, miss. Shall I ask Elijah to make a start on the garden?"

"Where all the lilacs grow."

Lilac couldn't help thinking wistfully that she would not now see them when they bloomed again in the spring. She would return to London and write immediately to Chance telling him that she had altered her mind about marriage. That would spare him the embarrassment of jilting her. She would have to guard her behaviour when she saw him again. He was a man who noticed the way in which others acted and drew the correct conclusions.

The rest of the day passed more slowly and miserably than any since her grandmother's death. It was quite useless to remind herself she was not actually in love with Chance Harland, that she had accepted his offer because she was feeling lonely; and the proposal itself had taken her by surprise. The truth was he had been growing steadily more attractive in her eyes ever since she met him.

By the next day Lilac had made up her mind. She could no longer bear to remain in suspense. Chance was going to a sheep sale, which meant he would not be at home. She would write a letter and take it round there. That would let him down lightly and bring the farce of their engagement to an end. However, writing the letter proved difficult.

After several fruitless attempts, it finally read:

Dear Chance,
    Since we met I have had second thoughts about our proposed marriage. Though I am sensible of the honour you have paid me, I do feel that the difference in our ages, coupled with the difference in our outlook, would render any alliance between us unhappy. I have decided to return to London as planned, but I would be grateful if you would

not seek permission for us to wed. I thank you again and remain,

Your sincere friend,
Lilac Mary Morton.

The letter sealed, Lilac went out to the stable yard to tell Elijah to saddle Daisy. She found him deep in conversation with Alice though it was the latter who seemed to be doing most of the talking. She broke off as Lilac approached.

"Well, I can't neglect my work in order to chat with you," Alice exclaimed. "I been telling Elijah you wanted the lilacs made ready for the spring, miss."

"Aye, that she has," Elijah agreed.

"Saddle Daisy for me, please," Lilac said.

Despite her own feelings of unhappiness she could not help feeling amused at the blush on her maid's face. Whatever his shortcomings as a conversationalist, Elijah had plainly affected Alice, who scuttled indoors with the blush still on her cheek. Lilac hoped he would make an offer very soon, before they returned south and Alice decided it was her duty to stay with her mistress. Meanwhile, Daisy whickered her pleasure at the prospect of another canter in the fresh air. There was an extra pang in Lilac's heart at the thought that when she left she would have to leave Daisy too.

Harland House looked particularly handsome this morning, with the ivy changing from its summer green into the red and gold of autumn and smoke curling lazily from the chimneys.

John opened the front door and volunteered the information that the master was away from home.

"Yes, I know." Lilac took out the letter and gave it to the servant." I wish him to receive that as soon as he returns. It's extremely important."

"I'll see he gets it, miss." John took it from her and went inside.

Lilac stared after him for a moment, while conflicting thoughts struggled for mastery. She had certainly done the right thing, making it impossible for Chance not to call off the wedding; but there was a feeling of loss all the same. Now she would never know if he had intended to go through with the ceremony or not. Either course would have been intolerable, since it was as shaming to be married out of pity as to be jilted. No doubt Chance would be relieved at her decision; and, by the time he discovered she was aware of the truth, she would be gone. Her last act before taking leave of Mrs Ackroyd had been to extract a promise that she would not talk about Lilac's visit.

Lilac had nearly reached the crest of the moor when she saw a lone horseman galloping over the rise. Her heart jerked uncomfortably; but it wasn't Chance; not unless he had dyed his hair yellow and put on a uniform.

"Alfred." She gaped at him as he reached her. "What in the world are you doing here?"

"Scarlet fever," Alfred said. "How are you, Lilac? Splendid to run into you like this."

"Scarlet—? Why are you not on your way to India?" she demanded.

"Scarlet fever in the barracks," he explained. "A whole bunch of us have been held up until the next sailing. Pray don't be alarmed. Had the beastly thing when I was a child, but it was decided to hold back our entire detachment. Rather be safe than sorry, what?"

"But what in the world are you doing in Yorkshire?" she demanded. "Why aren't you in London?"

"Mama got a fit of the frights," he said. "She knows perfectly well I've had scarlet fever, but she thinks it's possible to catch it twice, so she packed me off to find out how you are coping."

"She knows that I'm here? Oh, yes, by now she would. It is very good of her to be concerned."

"Caused quite a flutter, your leaving so suddenly. Mama was always fond of you."

Mrs Watson's affections would quickly diminish when

she found out that her daughter's best friend was the child of a murderer, Lilac thought wryly.

"Anyway," Alfred continued, "she suggested that I travel up here and check on your well-being and thus avoid passing on the disease that I'm not going to get because I've already had it. She was in such a taking that if Amelia had not already been wed she would have barred me from the ceremony."

"Amelia is married then?"

"As arranged. Handsome couple they made. Wentworth wasn't in our detachment so he sailed as planned. Amelia follows next week."

Lilac had always expected to hear of the irrevocable end of her romantic dreams with a sharp pang, but to her surprise she felt nothing at all. The image of Lieutenant Peter Wentworth had grown steadily fainter and smaller in her mind, until now, trying to conjure up his features, she could only visualise him with red hair.

"How did you get here?" she asked.

"On the stage," Alfred said, grimacing slightly. "Deuced uncomfortable mode of transport and frightful company. I took a room at Keighley, enquired directions, hired a horse and came."

"I am very glad to see you, Alfred," she said sincerely.

Indeed his familiar face and manner mitigated the sad, lost feeling that had been creeping over her ever since she delivered the letter.

"I went to the house and some biblical fellow said you'd ridden out," Alfred was continuing. "I must say I was taken aback to find you without escort."

"They are not so bound by convention in these parts," Lilac told him.

"Wild kind of place." He glanced about him disparagingly. "I can see why the Sladens never troubled to come up here when their cousin died."

"It can be beautiful," Lilac said.

By this time both of them had dismounted and were walking their mounts over the rough grass.

"Did you find out about your grandparents?" He gave her an enquiring look.

Lilac nodded, her face clouding.

"I'm afraid it is perfectly dreadful," she said with a little quiver in her voice. "They were cold and horrible people, not from these parts at all. My poor mother was most unhappy here and—well, my father was never killed by savages at all."

"But Mrs Lameter always said—"

"It was just a tale she invented so that I would be proud of his memory," Lilac gulped.

"Then what did happen to him?" Aflred asked.

"He shot both his parents and was hanged for murder." Lilac bit her lip on a sob.

"I say." Alfred stopped dead, staring at her with concern. "I say, that is deuced bad luck."

"It's believed he was insane," Lilac said shakily. "My grandmother never wanted me to know, but I think she meant to tell the truth to any man who offered for me."

"Then that explains . . . " It was Alfred's turn to stop and bite his lip.

"Your friend, Lieutenant Wentworth, was going to offer for me. He was, wasn't he?"

"He never actually said," Alfred told her, "but after he met you he kept on talking about you, dragging your name into every sentence. I could have sworn he actually went to speak to your grandmother on the Sunday afternoon, but I daresay I got it wrong. I generally do."

"No, you didn't mistake," Lilac said. "Grandmother sent me out with Alice that afternoon. So I think he did call, and she told him."

"And then he married my sister. That was a coward's trick."

"One cannot blame him for shying off the daughter of a killer," Lilac said.

"So what are you going to do now?" He glanced at her.

"I don't know." The lost feeling was returning. "I shall go back to London and wait for my great-uncle to arrive, I suppose."

"You could always marry me," Alfred said manfully. "Feel it was my fault you met Wentworth in the first place. Willing to make amends."

"That's very sweet of you, Alfred." Lilac was torn between laughter and weeping. "But you don't seem to understand. I cannot possibly marry anybody. Certainly I could not risk having any children, lest they were to grow up like their grandfather."

"To tell you the truth," he confided. "I never cared much for young ones myself. Noisy little brats, most of them, forever wanting one to read them stories or play a game. Quite willing to forego that pleasure."

"You are not in the least in love with me," she protested.

"Very fond of you," he mumbled uncomfortably. "Sister's best friend, disappointed by my friend, alone in the world and all that. You are not wearing the willow for Wentworth, by chance? Not in love with anybody else?"

"Of course not," Lilac said vehemently, and burst into tears.

"Oh, come now. Whoa, there."

Alfred had both arms round her and was patting her back as if she were a fractious baby. It was a relief to cry. She indulged herself for a few minutes, her head pressed against his shoulder.

"Been a shock for you," Alfred said, producing a handkerchief. "All by yourself. Ought not to have let you come up here all by yourself."

"Nonsense, Alfred." Lilac blew her nose and dabbed at her eyes. "My comings and goings were not your concern, and it was something I had to discover sooner or later. It is very sweet of you to offer me marriage when you know all about my dreadful family history, but you don't really want to marry me at all. It would be very wrong of me to take advantage of your generosity—"

"Speaking of which," he broke in. "I've got some news to cheer you. I redeemed your jewellery and brought it with me, also the money you loaned me to pay off my debts. Brought everything with me."

"How on earth—? A horse. You gambled on a horse. Oh, Alfred."

"This one won," he said simply. "Glad to repay and share my winnings. Half each."

"I couldn't possibly—"

"Make me feel better if you won't marry me," he said. "Always useful to have a little something."

"For once I'm pleased you gambled," Lilac said.

"Won four thousand guineas, rank outsider," he said and beamed.

"What was its name?" She took Daisy's rein and continued to walk.

"Last Chance," Alfred said.

"Oh dear." Lilac found herself weeping all over again, while Alfred, anxiously keeping pace, assured her he was still very willing to be wed.

=17=

"IT'S STUPID FOR you to be lodging in Keighley when we have so many rooms here," Lilac protested.

"Not sure it would be the right course," Alfred objected. "Yourself unwed and also myself, so to speak."

"Nonsense. Alice and Fanny and Elijah are here, and we are already old friends. Why, I think of you as a brother, Alfred."

"If you're absolutely certain," he said. "Then I'll ride over and get my bags. Supposed to report back to barracks in two weeks, and then it's off to India. If you're going home we could travel together."

She nodded thinking, not of the pleasure of Alfred's company, but of the extra week in Yorkshire. She would have time to leave instructions about the garden, and Elijah might get to the point of offering for Alice. That settled, Alfred rode off again, informing her he would stay overnight in Keighley and transfer to Sladen Hall the following morning.

By now Chance would surely have returned from the sheep sale and read her letter. Lilac had a picture in her mind of his crumpling the paper into a ball, flinging himself on his horse and galloping across the moor to inform her he refused to accept her decision but would marry her if he had to drag her up the aisle. It being real life, however, nothing of the sort would happen. Chance had not intended to go through with the wedding anyway, she told herself, while also telling herself she was relieved he had made no fuss.

Still, the sound of a horse clip-clopping up to the front door sent her out into the hall before any of the servants could get there. It was Nathan, who merely touched his cap and handed her a sealed letter before riding down the drive again. Lilac closed the door and took the letter up to her room. Her hand trembled as she kindled an extra lamp and broke the seal.

> Dear Miss Lilac,
> Your letter was delivered to me. Naturally I will abide my your decision, though I do express my regrets at your making it. May I wish you every happiness in the future?
> Your sincere friend,
> Chance Harland.

The formal words were like a dousing of cold water. He had accepted her rejection without one word of argument. He was probably relieved because he was spared the necessity of backing out himself. It would all work most conveniently now with no embarrassment on either side. Lilac wished she could indulge herself in another fit of weeping, but her eyes remained dry. She was conscious only of a hollow, disappointed feeling superseding every other emotion.

It was unlikely she would meet Chance again as he would undoubtedly find occupation that kept him away from the vicinity until she had returned south. She would not see his foxfire head, his bronze eyes with their dancing flecks of gold, nor hear his voice teasing her about the difference in their ages. With the letter still clutched in her hand Lilac met her own eyes in the looking glass.

"I believe I have begun to fall in love with Chance Harland," she said aloud with dismay.

She had imagined her acceptance of his proposal had

been based upon a feeling of friendship and the desire to replace the loneliness caused by Lieutenant Wentworth's defection, but the regrets flooding into the hollow space within her now were regrets for a lover lost.

Lilac sternly reminded herself that, but a brief time before, she had imagined herself in love with Peter Wentworth. Now she felt actual relief nothing had come of it. She could fall out of love with Chance Harland just as easily, if she set her mind to it. Indeed, from now on she had best accustom herself to the possibility that she would never marry. She would feel obliged to tell any prospective suitor the truth about her father. Very few men were willing to take such a risk, unless they were so unattractive that they were desperate for any wife you would have them. It was a dismal prospect.

In the morning Alice brought Lilac's coffee and the news that Alfred had arrived.

"I only 'opes as Mr Harland understands 'e's an old friend and there aint no funny business," she remarked.

"It doesn't matter what Mr Harland thinks," Lilac said, sipping her drink. "I am not going to marry him."

"Not marry 'im?" Alice stared at her in consternation. "Whatever are you saying, miss?"

"Alice, sit down for a moment." Lilac patted the edge of the bed. "I have discovered something about my family that's very shocking, and you have the right to know of it."

"Not if you don't want to tell me," Alice said staunchly. "Family affairs is private."

"My grandmother believed that and she would have done better to be open. Alice, my father was not killed by the Indians in America. He never reached America at all."

"Why, miss, whatever are you saying?" Alice gasped.

"He shot and killed both his parents and was hanged for it," Lilac said. "It was before I was born, and my mother went back to London where it was given out that he had been killed by savages. His surname is not an uncommon one, and news travelled more slowly in those days. After my mother died my grandmother kept up the story; but it was a fiction, Alice. Robert Morton was insane, and they hanged him."

"Oh, Miss Lilac, that's dreadful," Alice said. Her rosy face had paled.

"Fanny and Elijah know about it though they were only children when it happened, but Mr Harland made them promise to say nothing out of consideration for my feelings. That was really why he offered me marriage. He wished me to be away from this district before I found out the truth, and our engagement necessitated my return to London. He never would have gone through with the ceremony."

"Are you sure, Miss? He seems like a man of his word to me."

"That is his answer to my own note in which I broke off the engagement." Lilac handed it to her.

Alice read it slowly, silently shaping each word. When she looked up there were tears in her eyes.

"That's awful, miss," she said chokingly. "Oh, I am ever so sorry."

"It will all be for the best, you will see," Lilac said, more cheerfully than she felt. "If you and Elijah wed—"

"Oh, no, miss." Alice spoke firmly. "That's not to be thought of now, not after this."

"I wouldn't dream of spoiling your happiness."

"And I wouldn't dream of leaving you, miss, until I saw you nicely settled with a good man."

"Perhaps Elijah could come to London?" Lilac said, hopefully.

"No, miss." Alice shook her head. "It wouldn't do for 'im. 'E'd be out of place in a city. It wouldn't suit. Anyway, 'e's not made any offer yet. Just started working up to it so to speak, so there's no 'arm done. If it falls out that you get a good offer from a gentleman what don't care about fathers that's a different kettle of fish. Then we'll see about Elijah.

But leave you now I will not—not if I was to be torn limb from limb for it; and that's God's truth."

"Oh, Alice." Lilac embraced her impulsively. "You are a good friend."

"I 'ope not, miss," Alice said, shocked. "I 'ope I know my place better than that. But I'll not run off and wed until you're matched up, and that's my last word on the subject."

Whereupon she hugged Lilac fiercely and rustled out to the linen closet and could be heard the rest of the morning wreaking her pent-up feelings upon the unoffending linen.

Lilac entered the drawing room to find Alfred finishing a substantial breakfast.

"Dining room's being scrubbed out," he said by way of explaining his presence.

"I'm afraid a great deal requires to be done still," Lilac said.

"Place is pretty run down," he agreed. "I think Sladen ought to have warned me, but he may not have known. Never came near the house, he or his parents."

"I have enjoyed renovating it," she protested. "There is not very much to do in these parts."

"You got engaged," he said with a hint of reproach. "None of my business, but you might have told me before I made a fool of myself."

"Alice mentioned it, I suppose?" Lilac sighed. "I would have told you, Alfred. As it happens, I am now no longer engaged. I prefer not to go into details."

"No need. Understand perfectly." Alfred had coloured bright red. "Still available, you know, if you should change your mind. It would please my commanding officer no end."

"That's very kind of you, Alfred, but I am quite certain I won't change my mind. Now may we drop the subject?"

"Only too happy. What would you like to talk about?" He set down his cup and looked expectant.

"Come and walk round the garden with me," she invited. "I know I am leaving soon, but I want to begin clearing the garden for the next tenants. There is a particular spot that will be lovely when the spring comes. The lilacs are dying now, but if they can be trimmed and the weeds cleared they will be magnificent."

Alfred mumbled that gardening was not his strong point but allowed himself to be dragged out-of-doors, where he walked with some trepidation through the tangled paths.

"Not that I'm squeamish, mind," he said when she entreated him to hurry up. "Only, nature in the wild generally contains insects, adders, and the like. Not to mention thorns." He sucked tenderly at a scratch on his hand.

"What a baby you are," Lilac scolded. "I don't know how you will contrive when you are faced with real danger."

"Probably be a hero," he said. "Family tradition."

"And a happier one that mine," she said, sadness filling her again.

"Been thinking about that." Alfred circumnavigated a fallen log. "Seems to me you ought to look into the matter more closely. There could be extenuating circumstances, you know."

"The Mortons were fanatically religious," Lilac said. "I don't think that counts as an extenuating circumstance."

"Perhaps you're right. Sleeping dogs . . . I say. One can smell the lilac from here."

"Think how it will be when it's in bloom," she said. "Oh, I won't be here, but I like to think that someone else will get pleasure from it. I don't believe the Mortons left very happy memories in these parts. My mother used to come here. Chan—Mr Harland was a boy then, but he said she used often to walk out on the moor before I was born. She was very fond of this spot, and asked Mark Sladen's permission to come here now and then."

"And she named you Lilac," Alfred said.

"Just before she died. I suppose she wanted to remember the one place where she had contrived to get away from her parents-in-law and be content for a little space. I shall tell Elijah to begin clearing and pruning it at once."

"Stage leaves in ten days," Alfred reminded her. "I reserved three seats. Have you thought what you mean to do when you get back."

"I will stay and keep house for my great-uncle if he's home, I suppose," Lilac told him. "If he has not been contacted yet I will wait. At least your winnings mean I won't have to seek a position."

"If you'd entrust them to me, I could possibly double them in a few days."

"Or lose the lot. No, thank you, Alfred," Lilac said firmly. "I am quite happy with what I have and very grateful to you for paying me back so quickly."

"How about a gallop?" he suggested.

"Why not?" She answered with equal brightness. On horseback there was little leisure for brooding over what might have been.

"On horseback I'm less likely to get scratched to death," Alfred followed her to the house, relief in his good-natured face. As they mounted up he asked, "Is that one of the Sladen horses?"

"The Sladen stables consist of Pegasus, who is an elderly actor of a nag, and a foal too young to be ridden," Lilac said crisply. "Daisy was lent to me by Mr Harland. Elijah will take her back to him when we leave."

"That was kind of him," Alfred remarked.

"Yes, it was." Not wanting to discuss Chance Harland's kindness at that moment, Lilac tapped the mare into a trot.

"Like the end of the world," Alfred commented, when they were clear of the grounds.

"But beautiful." Lilac waved her arm towards the distant crags.

"Where did the Mortons live?"

"Over there. It is property belonging to Mr Harland. They rented it, but since the murder it has stood empty. I went over the house before I discovered the real story. It has a cold, bleak atmosphere."

As she spoke she wondered briefly in which of the rooms Robert Morton had drawn his gun on his parents and who had found them. Had it been her mother, returning from one of her lonely rambles on the moor? To know such details was completely useless. It was like probing a sore tooth with one's tongue.

"You don't wish to ride in that direction, do you?" she asked sharply.

"Lord, no. Far too upsetting for you," Alfred said kindly. "Trouble is, where does one ride in these parts? All looks the same to me, and the wind is biting."

"South is Oxenhope and over there one comes to Haworth and Stanmore," she explained. "I'm afraid there is a dearth of lively society, but people hereabouts make their own pleasures."

"Where does this Mr Harland live?"

"Down there. The house among the trees."

Pointing, she found herself straining her eyes to see if anyone moved in the driveway or on the lawn; but they were too far distant to see. Chance had probably ridden out on his normal, everyday business. The prospect of meeting him was remote, but the mere possibility made her nervous. If she never saw him again he would be much easier to forget.

"Make a splendid racecourse up here," Alfred said wistfully.

"Alfred, I have been thinking," she said impulsively. "We have ten days before the stage goes to London. Since I came into Yorkshire I have been nowhere. Why cannot we stay in York for a few days? I believe it is a vastly entertaining city."

"Without chaperone? And you are not out," he began doubtfully.

"Oh, fiddlesticks," she returned impatiently. "We are

without chaperonage here, and who is to know I am not out? Alfred, we could go as an engaged couple—"

"You mean you're accepting my offer?"

"No, of course not, so you need not struggle to conceal your dismay," she chided. "We could stay in separate rooms, of course. And I would have Alice with me. Or we could pass as cousins. Now, nobody could object to that. It would be far more lively for you than remaining here."

She knew from the look on his face that she had won her point. For her own part, she wanted only to put space between Chance Harland and herself.

=18=

"I HAD NOT realised that York was so large," said Lilac with interest.

They had travelled via the stage at Keighley, Elijah accompanying them and Alice riding pillion behind him so that he could return with the other horses. It would be the last time she would ride Daisy. She had instructed Elijah to take the horse back to Harland House. Alfred had left his hired mount at the livery stables and with an air of martyrdom accompanied the two women in the coach.

"We were fortunate to obtain accommodation," he said now. "The place is becoming quite fashionable though I doubt if it could ever compete with Brighton. I cannot see Prinny spending his holidays so far north."

"Perhaps you ought to recommend it to your friends. Then the prince would come to hear about it and desert Brighton," Lilac joked.

It had been an excellent notion to come. The change of scene alone held her interest. It was now possible to go for nearly an hour at a time without thinking of Chance Harland, though they had been there only two days. The inn at which they had taken lodging was a handsome one, and it was apparently acceptable for two cousins to stay at the same hostelry.

"Splendid racecourse here," Alfred said, giving her a hopeful glance.

"No, Alfred." Lilac spoke with almost maternal firmness. "Where is the sense in wasting your money and getting into debt again? It would be foolish when you are so near to rejoining your regiment."

"Might increase my money," he muttered somewhat sulkily.

"And I still have a great deal of exploring to get through," Lilac continued.

Alfred stifled a sigh. He had not expected his companion to be quite so determined to see every single thing there was to be seen. It involved a great deal of walking and poring over guidebooks. He had not expected Lilac to be so hungry for culture.

"We have seen the Minster and the Shambles and Clifford's Tower," Lilac was saying. "Did you know it is possible to walk right round the walls?"

"Better not," he advised hastily. "Terribly fatiguing, you know?"

Lilac's turn to stifle a sigh. Alfred was a dear, but he completely failed to understand that she wanted to be fatigued. She wanted to be so tired she fell asleep without dreaming of a tall man with dark red hair chasing her over a darkling moor while she longed to turn and ride to meet her pursuer. "A long walk would do you the world of good," she said firmly.

"Cold up above everything," he objected.

"There are steps at intervals," she persisted. "We need not complete the entire circle."

"If you're going climbing up them walls," Alice put in from behind, "you'll 'ave to hexcuse me, Miss Lilac. Never 'ad no 'ead for 'eights, never in me born days."

"There, you see," Alfred was beginning, but Lilac broke in.

"Then Alice may go back to the hotel. Come along, Alfred."

She headed purposefully for the nearest flight of steps. Alfred refrained from casting his eyes up to Heaven and manfully followed her.

It was certainly breezy on the guarded parapet, but the

view was breathtaking. Roofs and spires unfolded beneath, and the river shone silver in the distance. Lilac walked briskly, her escort following at a slower pace.

"Surely it's Alfred Watson?" An elderly lady coming towards them had paused, her voice expressing pleased surprise.

"Mrs Fenwick! How d'ye do, ma'am? I didn't know you lived hereabouts." Alfred too sounded pleased.

"My dear boy, I don't," she returned. My niece is coming out, and as my poor sister died five years ago somebody has to act hostess for my brother-in-law. I am here for a month. You have not met my niece? Lavinia, my sweet. This is Lieutenant Alfred Watson, whose mama went to school with me though I absolutely refuse to tell you how long ago that was."

"Five years at most," Alfred said gallantly.

"Still as charming," Mrs Fenwick said, tapping him on the arm. "May I introduce my niece, Miss Lavina Beagle?"

A plump, pretty girl at the lady's side smiled and bobbed a curtsey.

"Miss Beagle. Oh, forgive me." He realised that Lilac was standing by looking awkward. "My . . . distant cousin, Miss Lilac Morton."

"Also visiting?" Mrs Fenwick shot an inquisitive glance.

"I have been in poor health, ma'am," Lilac invented rapidly. "Scarlet fever, but now quite recovered."

"Dear me." There was the faintest motion of withdrawal.

"Oh, I am completely recovered now," Lilac said hastily. "Lieutenant Watson was staying here and kindly agreed to act as escort while I indulged myself in a little exploring. My maid has no head for heights, so I sent her away."

"You are here with only a maid? That is marvellously unconventional of you." Her expression was still slightly bemused.

"I am not well acquainted with anybody in the north," Lilac said. "That is why I was so grateful when Mrs Watson suggested that Alfred escort me. Amelia and I were at school together."

"Ah, I see." Mrs Fenwick looked slightly happier. "I had not heard of cousins named Morton. But I am sure we are all related in one way or another. And how are you two young people spending your time?"

"Mainly walking," Alfred said gloomily.

"As I have no older chaperone I cannot go out into society," Lilac said.

"But a private party, surely, would be possible? As it happens, I am holding a modest evening tonight. Nothing elaborate. Lavinia is so very popular that I am forced to limit her activities else she would be quite exhausted, but you could both attend such a tiny function without any offence of propriety."

Lilac hesitated. The prospect of a party was nice, but she was not certain if she could evade the inevitable questions concerning her presence in Yorkshire. It would be dreadful if she were to meet somebody who knew the history of the Mortons.

"If Miss Morton is willing," Alfred said, "I believe we would like to come very much."

Lilac found herself nodding and smiling. Alfred had been very kind, after all; and there was only a faint chance that anyone would connect Miss Morton from London who was recuperating from scarlet fever with a man called Robert Morton, hanged nearly twenty years before.

"Tonight at ten? I will send a linkboy to guide the way. At which hotel— Ah, an excellent place." She beamed as Alfred told her. "It is becoming de rigueur for people to stay at public inns, I believe. They have improved tremendously since I was a girl."

"I look forward to this evening, ma'am. Miss Beagle." Alfred bowed politely and they walked on.

"I gather the lady is an old friend of your family," Lilac said.

"Beg pardon?" Alfred had turned to gaze after Lavinia.

He blinked, then nodded. "Charming woman. Always used to give me a sovereign when she saw me. Pretty niece, don't you think?"

"I perceive that *you* think so," Lilac said, amused. "Pray don't forget that you are soon returning south."

"But one social engagement won't hurt. Are you sure that you really want to walk round the entire city? Wouldn't you care to rest for the dancing this evening?"

"I don't intend to dance," Lilac said, then relented. "We will walk to the next flight of steps and then descend. I think I will buy myself a dress for this evening. I have nothing suitable for a young lady who is supposed to have come out."

"She didn't ask."

"Obviously she assumed it. No girl who was not yet out would be staying at an hotel with a gentleman."

"Supposed to be cousins," he reminded her.

"We had better be prepared to be a little more specific," Lilac warned. "Can you invent an aunt once removed on your father's side or something? I believe your reputation as well as mine would suffer were it to become known that we were not related at all. I am not so concerned for my own since I am not in the market for a husband, but I am exceedingly fond of you, Alfred—."

"But not sufficiently fond to accept my proposal, eh?" Alfred was beginning to look rather alarmed.

"Pray don't fret." Lilac shot him a mischievous glance. "I won't retract my refusal, so you are safe to lose your heart to Miss Lavinia Beagle."

"Would please my commanding officer, you know," Alfred said, going slightly pink.

And I have nobody to please except myself, Lilac thought. It is in the last degree unlikely that any gentleman will offer for me when he is informed of my history, and it would be very wrong to conceal it as Grandmother did. I must resign myself to the probability that I will never wed, but will end my days as housekeeper to Uncle Philip when he is too old to go travelling any longer.

At least she would contrive to look her best that evening, she decided. As it had clearly been taken for granted that she was already out, she could relinquish the delicate pastels that were suitable for very young girls and indulge herself in something more sophisticated.

She found the perfect dress that afternoon when, having left Alfred to put his feet up, she sallied forth with Alice in the hope of buying something ready-made. The narrow skirt and low-cut bodice were of midnight blue velvet, flounced at hem and shoulders, and daringly unadorned. She had brought the redeemed jewels with her and would wear the topaz earrings. The price was more than she had anticipated, but the gown fitted her as if it had been made for her.

Looking at herself in the long pier glass in the tiny fitting room, she was filled with a sudden recklessness. If she were destined to end her days as a spinster that didn't mean she had to be a dowdy one. She might even become a mysterious lady of whom others whispered that she as an adventuress and had never married because of some romantic secret in her past. Paying for the gown, she felt sympathy for her grandmother for the first time. Barbara Lameter had also invented a story, because the truth was too painful to live with.

During her explorations, Lilac had carefully avoided the streets that radiated from the looming bulk of the gaol. One part of her wanted to make enquiries so that she would know the full story, but another part of her shrank from that knowledge. Whatever the circumstances, nothing could alter the fact that Robert Morton had killed his parents and nobody would wish to risk marrying her in consequence.

"You look ever so grand, miss," Alice complimented when she was finally dressed. "Anyone'd take you for at least twenty."

"Oh, I hope so," Lilac said.

"If not twenty-one," Alice added. "Elegant is the word."

With her hair swept high on her head and the long earrings emphasising her slender neck, she did have a new maturity. It was in her eyes too, she thought. It was impossible to learn an unpleasant truth and remain a child.

Alfred, looking happier since the cancellation of any further walking, gave her an approving smile as he handed her up to the rented carriage. "You look very—"

"Elegant?"

"Deuced elegant. Not ashamed to be complimentary when occasion calls. Deuced elegant. I won't be surprised if you don't make a conquest, you know."

"It will do me little good," she said wryly, "since my family would deter any potential suitors."

"Absolutely necessary to tell them, I suppose?"

"Not unless someone offers for me, and I shall take good care that none of my friendships develop to that stage."

"Deuced pity," he said warmly.

"I shall learn to live with it," she said lightly. "Now, do remember that your father had an aunt who was your uncle's cousin."

"What does that make us?" he enquired.

"Relatives, I suppose," Lilac said impatiently. "There is no need to go into detail about our exact degree of cousinship, you know. Probably nobody will ask anyway."

The linkboy was running ahead of the slow-moving vehicle, his flaring torch held high. Lilac looked out into the dark street and wondered suddenly how it would be to sit in the intimacy of this carriage with a man she loved, instead of with Alfred Watson. It was a fruitless thought because she had never really loved Peter Wentworth at all, and she had only just begun to love Chance Harland. Easier to break a habit at the beginning, she told herself firmly.

"This evening will make a pleasant change for you, Alfred, she said aloud with deliberate brightness."

The house to which they had been invited proved to be a large, handsome one set in a tree-lined square.

"This is almost like London," Alfred said approvingly, as they went up the steps.

But it won't be possible to look out of the windows and see the sweeping grandeur of the moor, Lilac thought, with the high crags rising into the sky and the beck flooded when the rains came.

"Merely a modest gathering of friends," Mrs Fenwick said, rustling to meet them. "Miss Morton, you look extremely á la mode. Such a pleasure to see the latest fashions up in the barbaric north. Alfred—for I have known you a very long time—you must persuade my foolish niece that she looks delightful in pink. She is dreadfully modest."

"Delighted, ma'am," said Alfred promptly disappearing in the direction of the pink-clad Miss Beagle.

"Let me see to whom you might like to be introduced, my dear." Mrs Fenwick's eyes widened as Lilac removed her cloak, but she regained her hostess smile at once. "The younger gentlemen are all wild for dear Lavinia, but there must be—ah, yes."

"My dear ma'am, there is not the least need to put yourself to trouble—"

Lilac's voice trailed into silence as Mrs Fenwick pounced upon the tall gentleman just entering. Despite the conventional evening attire and a cravat that must have taken hours to achieve, he brought something wild and untamed into the overheated room.

"Mr Harland, allow me to present you to Miss Lilac Morton," Mrs Fenwick was saying. "She is staying with her cousin, recuperating after an illness, though I am happy to say she is quite recovered now. Miss Morton, Mr Chance Harland is a gentleman of whom we see all too little, for he buries himself on his moorland property."

"Miss Morton and I are slightly acquainted already," Chance said smoothly. "You did not mention that your cousin was with you."

"I fear he will be a somewhat neglectful one," Mrs Fenwick said merrily, "for I see him leading Lavinia out for the measure. As you are acquainted I will leave you to renew. I must check on the supper."

She looked rather helplessly from one to the other and rustled away again.

"Elijah told me you were in York," Chance said. "I am delighted to find that you were not mistaken in the depth of Lieutenant Wentworth's affection for you."

"Who?" Lilac followed his nod and shook her head. "Oh, that is not Peter Wentworth. That is—"

"Another officer evidently. I congratulate you on the number of your military acquaintances."

"He is not—"

"Not your cousin? I do believe you mentioned you had only a great-uncle left in the world. Or is he quite extraordinarily youthful for his years?"

"That is Alfred," Lilac said weakly.

"Alfred. Alfred who is not your cousin?"

"He is a friend of mine. As a matter of fact, he is—"

"The reason you broke off your engagement to me, I presume. I was informed you had been seen embracing an officer out on the moor."

"I did no such thing," Lilac began indignantly. "He was trying to calm my weeping, that's all."

"You really don't owe me any explanation, you know," Chance said, hard-eyed. "I was very naive to imagine that my offer could possibly compete with the excitement of being courted by an officer."

He was angry. Lilac stared at him, wondering why since Alfred's arrival had spared Chance the necessity of jilting her.

"Alfred," she said in a small voice, "is Amelia's brother. He came up with my—he came to find out how I was. His departure has been delayed for a brief period, and he decided to escort me back to London."

"When he had finished flaunting you round York, I suppose."

"Flaunting!" Her voice rose. "I wished to visit York before I returned south. Alice came with us—but surely Elijah told you?"

"Elijah answers questions. I have never known him to volunteer information. As I said, it really is none of my affair."

"No, it isn't, is it?" she flashed, stung by the contempt in his tone.

"I'm sure you will excuse me. I see some people I know." He gave her the coldest of bows and turned away.

Unexpected tears pricked her eyes. Chance treated her as if she had offended him, when all she had done was to save him from embarrassment and trouble. Men, all men in fact, were quite impossible. She swallowed hard and cast such a brilliant smile upon a gentleman on his way to the card tables that he changed direction and veered towards her.

"This being an informal occasion, I will dispense with ceremony," he said pleasantly. "I am Henry Beagle, and you must be one of my daughter's friends."

"You are Lavinia's father." She shook hands. "I'm afraid I am scarcely acquainted with Miss Beagle, sir. My cousin, Lieutenant Watson, is an old friend of Mrs Fenwick. She and his mama attended the same school, and, as we were staying the district, she invited us this evening. My name is Lilac Morton."

"Morton?" He wrinkled his brow. "There was a Morton. I doubt there is any connection."

"Robert Morton?" Lilac had tensed.

"A very unpleasant man, my dear. Murdered his own parents. Not a subject to be discussed with young ladies."

"As a matter of fact," Lilac said, somewhat breathlessly, "I understand he was a distant relative of mine—by marriage. Naturally I was curious about the—There were mitigating circumstances, I daresay?"

177

"I am sorry to hear that he was ever any connection," Mr Beagle said, shaking his head. "He was insane, you know. Completely insane, religious mania. Wished to be a missionary, but the bishop wisely rejected his application. He took it into his head that his parents were in league with the powers of darkness to prevent his fulfilling his vocation and killed them both. He would probably have killed his wife too, but she was out on the moors at the time and so escaped. A farmhand discovered the bodies, but by then Morton had ridden to give himself up to the authorities. He was convinced that, having killed his parents, he would be allowed to go as a missionary. I hope you are not close related, my dear."

"Only distantly," Lilac said. She felt faint and sick.

"Ah, most families have their burdens to bear. Now, I do not dance, but may I offer you some refreshment? My sister-in-law manages these affairs splendidly."

"Thank you."

She accepted his arm and moved with him into the inner room where the tables had been set out. He was a hospitable gentleman who would be distressed if he were to learn that he had been talking to Robert Morton's daughter. For the rest of her life she would feel like this, she thought, as the cold winds of loneliness shivered through her beneath the clinging velvet gown.

=== 19 ===

NEVER IN HER life had Lilac endured such an interminable evening. Mr Beagle brought her supper, then began to tell her about the virtues of his late wife in such detail that, long before she had eaten her dessert, Lilac felt as if she were intimately acquainted with the lady. From time to time she caught a glimpse of Chance Harland dancing with one partner after another, not taking the least notice of her. One could not blame him for considering her a sad flirt, she reflected, smiling as her host droned on.

After Mr Beagle came a flushed and excited Alfred to inform her that he had arranged to go riding with Miss Lavinia the following day.

"Deuced splendid girl," he confided. "Very interested in horses. I must say I'm awfully grateful to you for turning down my offer of marriage."

Despite her misery, Lilac had to smile at the thought of having made him happy by a refusal rather than an acceptance.

"I wish you joy," she responded. "Indeed I do. A match would delight your commanding officer, and she clearly comes from a good family."

"A mite premature to make firm plans," he demurred, "but your sentiments are mine exactly. I don't suppose you'd care to dance?"

"You are correct, Alfred." She held the smile in place by an effort of will. "To tell you the honest truth I am dropping with weariness, and think I ought to make my apologies and leave. There is no need for you to escort me. I am quite capable of sitting in a coach as it drives towards the hotel."

"Nonsense, couldn't possibly allow a lady to go home unescorted," Alfred began.

"You are perfectly right, Lieutenant," a voice interrupted. Chance Harland had strolled up and was bowing. "However, the lady has an escort so you need not inconvenience yourself."

"That's most civil of you, sir, but I hardly think—"

"I know Mr Harland," Lilac said.

"Harland? The—"

"The man your . . . cousin has recently jilted. Or perhaps she has not yet told you about that. Never mind. She will explain it all another time I'm sure. Did you have a wrap, Miss Morton?"

Mutely she gave in to him: felt his hands briefly on her shoulders as he draped her wrap over her, then went meekly to bid her hostess good-night while Alfred gaped.

"Very happy to have made your acquaintance, Miss Morton," Mrs Fenwick said. "Pleasant for you to have a friend in these parts after all. We are having a little riding expedition tomorrow, most glad if you could join us, but after your illness—most unpleasant, scarlet fever. I am astonished that your hair was not cut to alleviate the fever."

"It was," said Chance. "Miss Morton wears a wig."

"Oh, my dear. How unfortunate." Mrs Fenwick looked as if she were liking her guest better all the time.

"We don't often mention it," Chance said. "We shall use my coach."

Somehow or other Lilac found herself in a plush-upholstered seat with Chance opposite her.

"You don't keep a carriage," she said stupidly.

"In York I do," Chance said.

"And you genuinely didn't know that I was here?"

"Had I known I would not have come," he said. "I am not in the habit of chasing where I am not wanted."

"Then I don't understand why you are driving me back to the hotel."

"Because I am a trifle puzzled as to why you allow your best friend's brother to stay at the same hotel, to escort you to an evening function, and then display not the least chagrin at his pursuit of another young lady."

"Alfred is merely a friend. I tried to explain who he was, but you were not in a humour to listen," she said. "We came to York because I wished to see the city before I returned to London. We decided to call ourselves cousins so as not to outrage convention."

"Wearing that dress outrages it quite sufficiently," he said dryly.

"It is a beautiful dress," Lilac said indignantly. "It makes me look twenty-one at least."

"Positively elderly," he agreed. "You look as if you are embarking on a career as an adventuress."

"Which is not your concern as we are not going to be wed."

"Because our tastes differ, as you put in your letter. I believed that Lieutenant Wentworth had rushed up to the north in search of you and so, naturally, accepted your decision. Now it begins to look as if I haven't even been thrown over for Alfred Watson."

"I found out about my father," she said, throwing pretence to the winds. "I realised at once that your efforts to send me back to London were to prevent my finding out."

"The story is an ugly one," he said, grown suddenly sombre. "You were happier not knowing it."

"Then I realised that after I had returned to London you would find means to break off the engagement. So I decided to spare you the embarrassment."

"You consider my offer of marriage was a ploy designed to keep you from finding out about your father. Is that it?"

"Not exactly a ploy," she faltered. "Indeed, I think it most kind in you to wish to spare me unhappiness, but obviously you could not have gone through with the ceremony. Even if you were willing to take the risk of wedding the daughter of . . . Well, sooner or later I would have been bound to find out about it. Assuming we had continued to live in that district."

"By then you might have been secure and happy enough not to be crushed by such information," he said.

"You mean that you really would have married me?" Lilac sat staring at him in the semi-gloom.

"It seemed the sensible course of action," Chance said.

"But it would have been a terrible risk," she protested. "I don't wish to be indelicate. I know very little about these things, but surely mental defectiveness can be inherited?"

"Sometimes. It is not always so."

"It is my opinion," she said unsteadily, "that the older Mortons were a little mad too. They were fanatics, and they infected their son. It would be most foolish for any man to seek to wed me knowing that."

"A man who loved you would gladly take the risk," he said.

"I suppose—Loved?"

"Did you imagine that I offered you marriage as a social duty?" Chance enquired. "I will be honest and confess that when we first met I was of the opinion you were a spoiled minx who had come into Yorkshire with the intention of stirring up as much trouble as possible. I quickly realised that you had never been told the truth, and I didn't want you to be hurt. I was falling wildly in love with you by then, you see. I was quite astonished at the strength of my own feelings."

"You did not seem so."

"I warned you that I am not a demonstrative man," he said impatiently. "You must remember too that I am somewhat more experienced than you are. It was not my desire to frighten you away with too intense a proof of my loving."

"And you really would have gone through with it?"

"I would not have packed you off to London in the

expectation of a wedding ceremony only to call it off at the last minute," he said.

"Then you really did love me," Lilac said slowly.

"What is this 'did' and 'would have'?" he demanded. "Now that we are under no misapprehension about our respective intentions, the arrangements can go on as planned."

He had not yet touched her, but she felt herself on fire with his presence.

"The risk—" she began.

"Is for me to fret about, Lilac. I promise you that I am sure of my own feelings."

"The thought of Robert Morton doesn't frighten you?"

"It requires two people to produce a child. From the very little I saw of your mother she struck me as charming and perfectly normal. I also believe in the power of the environment. You were reared by your grandmother who may have been wrong to conceal the truth from you but was not, from what you have told me, fanatical."

"No, she was not," Lilac said.

Her mind was whirling. That Chance could have fallen in love with her was a possibility she had not seriously considered. She had believed his offer sprang from kindness.

"I suggest that we return to our respective homes tomorrow and that the wedding arrangements continue as we planned," he said.

They had reached the hotel. As the carriage stopped, Chance leaned forward and kissed her lightly and swiftly on the lips.

There was a smile in his voice as he said, "Now you are thoroughly compromised and will have to marry me in order to protect your social standing. I will call on you in the morning. The dress, by the by, is splendid. Mrs Fenwick was in agonies lest her niece be cast into the shade. Tomorrow, Lilac."

The coachman helped her to alight, and she went up the steps into the foyer as if she were walking on air.

"You look as if you 'ad a good time," Alice remarked, "though it's early yet. What 'appened?"

"I found out that I am truly in love," Lilac said, and hugged her.

"Lawks. Who is it now?"

"Mr Harland, of course. He was at the party, and he really means to wed me in spite of my father."

"Followed you, did 'e?" Alice looked impressed.

"It was coincidence. He thought I was marrying Alfred. Oh, it's a long tale. What matters is that he loves me sufficiently to take the risk."

Lilac ceased, her face paling, her hands clasping tightly together. For a long moment she and Alice stared at each other. Then Lilac sat down on the stool near the dressing table.

"And I love him too much to allow it," she said.

"Oh, Miss Lilac." Alice looked distressed.

"I really do love him," Lilac said as slowly as if she were tasting the words. "And when you love someone it isn't a lightsome thing. I can't let him take a wife who cannot risk having children. It would be abominably selfish of me."

"What are you going to do?" said Alice in a hushed tone.

"I have to think." Lilac pressed her hands to her temples. "We must leave at once. Tonight. He is calling upon me in the morning, so we must be well away by then. He will not call too early, I fancy. He will give me time to have my sleep out. Alfred will stay at the party until the last possible moment because he is greatly taken with Miss Beagle. In the morning he is going riding with her. He will not even realise that we are gone for several hours. I will pay the porter here to say nothing."

"But where are we going, Miss?" Alice said plaintively.

"First to Sladen Hall to pick up the rest of our things and then—" Lilac hesitated.

"If we go straight to London 'e'll follow us there," Alice

said. "Miss Lilac, are you certain sure you're doing the right thing?"

"I'm absolutely sure," Lilac said sombrely.

"Then where are we going?" Alice repeated.

"We will go north," Lilac said. "Alice, you must hurry down now and hire a coach. We will continue north."

"But north where, miss?" Alice demanded.

"Scotland," Lilac said.

"Scotland? Miss Lilac, we don't know anybody in Scotland," said Alice in horror. "Oh, I don't think you'd be comfortable in Scotland. They eat 'aggis there."

"It will only be for a few weeks," Lilac reassured her. "Thank heavens I have money to enable me to travel a little. After a few weeks we will return to London, and by then Mr Harland will have ceased looking for me."

"Are you sure?" Alice said.

Lilac reflected a moment longer, then nodded. Chance was proud. He would not persist in his suit if she contrived to vanish completely.

"Go down and get the porter to order a coach," she said, forcing briskness into her tone. "I will begin packing. You had best leave the money for our rooms here, and make sure that the porter says nothing should he be asked. Hurry now."

She gave Alice a little push, thinking that it would be the worst possible luck if Alfred were to come back while they were making preparations for departure. That she was doing the right thing she never doubted, but she wished she could find more joy in the doing of it.

= 20 =

"Lucky we managed to get 'old of a coach," Alice said. "At this time of night it weren't easy."

"You did very well, Alice." Lilac spoke wearily, leaning her head back against the padded seat.

She had been in a fever of indecision up to the last moment, wondering what she would say if Alfred were to return, hoping that Chance wouldn't follow them, hoping that he would. She was embarking on the right course. She knew it in her bones. She loved Chance, not in the shallow, infatuated way she had felt about Peter Wentworth, but with a love which made it impossible to place burdens upon the beloved. She wished she could feel differently, that she didn't have a conscience; but she was the product of Barbara Lameter's rearing.

"We will stay only a brief time at Sladen Hall," she warned. "You must pack up quickly, then we will make for Carlisle."

"Yes, miss," Alice said, her voice subdued.

Lilac felt another pang of compunction. Her decision had spoiled things for Alice too. Yet, it would be fruitless to try and persuade the maid to stay behind. Alice also had her principles.

They both dozed along the way, but as the coach lumbered onto the moor the jolting roused them. The coachman, who insisted on double fare before he would set out in the middle of the night, had slowed the horses to a walk. Through the windows Lilac could discern the waving fronds of bracken, the white silhouette of rock against the dark sky.

She had given careful directions to the driver and he seemed to be following them. He had whipped up the horses again and was speeding down the turf beyond which rose the walls of Sladen Hall. The coach lurched and tilted, and Alice screamed out. Her scream was cut short as the vehicle toppled sideways, the horses whinnying loudly above the sound of rushing water.

Suddenly, the door was where the roof had been, and water was jetting in at every crevice. The two of them had landed in a tangled heap. Alice pulled herself into a sitting position and began to wail loudly.

"The beck's in flood," said Lilac in something of a daze, sitting up just as a stream of water poured in from the opening door above.

The round moon of the driver's face appeared in the aperture. "Ma'am, are you hurt?" he shouted.

"No, I don't think so, only wet," Lilac said.

"I can make shift to haul you out," he said. "Coach is stuck fast though."

"Thank you. Alice, you follow me."

"Lilac was regaining her composure. Though the water was splashing in, it was clear they were not in imminent danger of drowning. The next few minutes were uncomfortable and undignified nonetheless. It took a deal of heaving on the part of both herself and the coachman before Alice was tugged out of the coach, like a cork from a bottle. Meanwhile, the water swirled below them, gleaming in the darkness.

"It comes to my waist," the coachman said, testing cautiously. "Lantern went out. Can you make for the bank while I see to the horses?"

"Yes, of course." Lilac slid down into the icy water and waded towards the rushes with Alice at her heels, clutching Lilac's shoulder.

The banks were steeper than she had expected, and her

feet sank deep into the mud. Tufts of grass broke off in her fingers as she finally pulled herself clear and landed on hands and knees on the higher ground.

"Oh, miss," Alice said quaveringly. "I thought as 'ow we was drowned dead."

"Not yet." Lilac struggled to her feet and watched the dark bulk of the coachman lead the horses up onto the bank.

"Coach is settling into the mud," he said.

"The house is not far. What about the luggage?"

"Tied on tight. Mind you, the water'll have seeped in."

She thought briefly and regretfully of her lovely, midnight blue dress, then lifted her chin.

"Elijah can get it at dawn. It is close to that now, surely. We'd better make straight for the house. Alice, do stop crying. You are not in the least hurt."

"Me innards," said Alice, sniffing loudly, "is probably destroyed."

Lilac's involuntary chuckle carried them forward. The walls of Sladen Hall had never seemed so welcoming. Sooner than she had hoped, her frantic hammering brought Elijah and Fanny to the door blinking sleep out of their eyes.

"The carriage overturned, and we fell in the beck," she said.

"Aye, I can see that," Elijah said.

"Then don't stand there like a great gorm," Alice exclaimed, her natural energy asserting itself.

"We shall all require hot drinks and probably baths too," Lilac said. "As soon as it's light, you must help to right the coach. The horses want rubbing down and stabling too. And you had best bring the luggage to the house as some of it is likely to be wetted."

All was suddenly bustle and movement, with the tear-stained Alice chiding Elijah and Fanny impartially. As a result, hot water appeared from nowhere in a very short space of time. By full dawn Lilac was clean and dry again, clad in her heavy travelling dress with her hair hanging in a damp tail down her back.

She huddled by the fire in the drawing room, trying to think clearly as she sipped the scalding chocolate that Fanny had produced. The carriage was undamaged. The driver and Elijah had gone down to inspect it and reported that it could be righted.

"But it'll take a day or two afore it dries out, ma'am," the driver informed her.

By that time Chance might have arrived, or Alfred.

"We shall have to ride," she said.

"Pegasus is slow and Daisy went back," Fanny reminded her. If the Yorkshire girl wondered at the comings and goings of the tenants she kept her curiosity to herself.

"What about the carriage horses? Would it be possible to hire them?"

"They pull coaches," the driver said, "not mounts for ladies."

"And there ain't no saddles," Alice added.

"So, for the moment, we must stay here."

Lilac kneaded her aching head with the tips of her fingers. This was a ridiculous and impossible situation.

She was behaving as if Chance Harland had the power to drag her screaming up the aisle and force her to wed him. The truth was she feared that if she saw him again, her resolution would falter.

"We had better wait then," she said slowly. "Get the carriage and horses out of sight, and if anyone calls we are not at home."

"Does that mean we ain't going to Scotland after all?" Alice said brightly.

"I don't know, Alice. I will be incapable of making firm plans until I have slept for several hours," Lilac answered wearily.

Her remark was the signal for more bustle. She kept her eyes open long enough to remove her shoes and was vaguely conscious of Alice piling blankets over her. Then Lilac fell into an exhausted sleep. When she woke it was past noon, and she was hungry.

Outside the window the sun was shining, and nearby trees waved in the breeze. For an instant, she forgot how unhappy she was. Then the reality of her situation rushed back into her mind, and the bright day was darkened. The money she had wouldn't last forever. Sooner or later she would have to go back to London. It had been a mistake to consider fleeing north when it would only cost more money.

"'ave you made up your mind what to do?" Alice enquired, coming in with a temptingly full plate.

"I begin to think that Scotland would be a mistake—but don't start thanking the Lord for it. It would be very childish of me to run away. We shall stay here until the coach is dried out, and then we shall travel to London. I will wait for Uncle Philip to arrive; and if Mr Harland does turn up here or there, I shall simply refuse to see him."

"Yes, Miss Lilac," Alice said.

"About Elijah—"

"We'll fret about that when the time comes," Alice said stolidly.

It was an enviable trait, to be in a position to put aside worries until a more convenient time. Lilac wished she were capable of doing the same. She had not faltered in her resolve, but her heart was sore, and she would have given much to have been able to indulge in a fit of tears. Instead, she applied herself to the chicken pie and vegetables and was rather ashamed of the heartiness of her appetite. Evidently, she was not destined to pine away even if her spirts were lower than they had ever been in her life. Lilac finished her meal and pushed back the blankets. It was foolish to mope about the house. She would walk in the garden for an hour and pay her last visit to the lilac garden.

Elijah had obviously been busy there. The paths were cleared of brambles and many of the lilac bushes, carefully pruned. In the spring the place would be a delight to the eye and the nose. It was not surprising that her mother had found refuge here from the cold, harsh home where her parents-in-law lived. She must have sensed the madness growing in her husband and feared it.

Lilac savored the last traces of sensuous perfume lingering over the newly dug earth, then wrapped her cloak more tightly round her shoulders and made her way back to the house. In the kitchen, the luggage was drying out in front of the range while the coachman regaled Fanny with an account of the time he had fought off a gang of highwaymen single-handed.

Elijah came across the stable-yard with one of the coach horses. Lilac stepped out to the cobbles and called to him.

"Thank you for making a start on the garden, Elijah. You have been working hard, I see."

"Aye, miss, that I have," he agreed. "I threw weeds on't midden and put box in't barn."

"What box?" she queried.

"Tin box, miss. It were dug up by me. I put it in't barn," he repeated.

"Was there anything in it?"

"I didn't look," Elijah said.

"Bring it to me in the drawing room." Lilac wondered what it was like to be so devoid of curiosity. Probably very restful.

There was no sign of Alice. She was probably lying down, recovering from the fright and wetting of the previous night. Alice had her own sorrow, Lilac remembered and wished there were some way of resolving it happily.

"This is't, miss," said Elijah, placing a rusted box on the table. "Old tinder box."

"Is it locked?" Lilac examined it curiously.

"Lid's jammed. Tha mun use a knife," he said, pulling out his own and prising up the lid. Inside was a small leather bag. Lilac drew it out and tugged the drawstrings loose. A few flakes of dried petals fluttered down to the tabletop.

"Now why would folks want t'bury dead flowers?" Elijah said, scratching his head.

Lilac plunged her hand into the bag. Her fingers closed on stiff paper; and, as she pulled it out, her mother's handwriting, faded and smudged, leapt to her eye.

"Thank you, Elijah. That will be all."

After he had gone, Lilac carried the paper to the window where the light was stronger. The message bore no salutation, but began abruptly.

"I don't know if anyone will ever read this letter; but perhaps one day, Mark, when the garden is being dug, you will find it and know that we did not love in vain. I lied to you, my dearest, when I told you that the child I carry is Robert's. The truth is that Robert never asserted his husbandly rights after we came to live in his parents' house. Even before that, he had taken me without joy and then prayed for forgiveness afterwards. He believes me to be almost two months nearer my time than I am. God knows what he will do when he realises the truth. He may not trouble to count. I pray he will not.

"There is something terribly wrong with my husband, Mark. I have tried not to notice it, but it frightens me more and more. I have written to my mother and begged her to come. You need not fear that I will ever reveal our secret— my secret, for you may never know unless you find this. What we did was very sinful. It was also very sweet, and I do not regret it as deeply as I ought. You will marry a fine young lady and forget about Mary Morton who walked in your garden. Whatever happens to me I will never lose the perfume of the lilacs. We crushed them as we lay and made a tiny Eden of our own. I will not seek you out again, nor return to our garden.

"If you find this you will know that I loved you,
Mary"

Mary Morton, gentle and pious, finding a few moments of happiness with a young man, then, tormented by her conscience, saying nothing. Not even when she lay dying had she dared to tell that her baby was the child of another man.

Lilac read the faded message through once again and was filled with anguish. Poor, foolish Mary, so concerned to protect her secret. She had never realised the harm her silence had caused.

"Robert Morton was not my father," Lilac said aloud.

The words liberated her. Suddenly she was hurrying out the door to the stable. The letter was still in her hand as she called to Elijah. "Saddle Pegasus. The broken saddle will do. Hurry."

Elijah shifted the straw he was sucking from one side of his mouth to the other and gave her a startled look but hastened to obey. Once mounted, Lilac held back only long enough to ask one question.

"Would you like to marry Alice?"

"Aye, miss, that I would," he said.

"Then go and ask her. Tell her that Miss Lilac said it was all right. Go on now."

"Yes, miss. That I will." Elijah answered, the straw falling from his lips as he beamed.

Lilac flicked Pegasus with her crop. "Pretend you're a racehorse today," she begged.

The old horse, perhaps moved by her urgency, proceeded to give an excellent imitation of a gallop. He had slowed down considerably, however, by the time they reached the gates of Harland House. Lilac slipped from the saddle and ran ahead, her face glowing as the door opened and Chance appeared on the threshold. The possibility that he might not have returned from York had not occurred to her. Still, her relief at the sight of him was immense.

"Oh, Chance. I am so glad you are home." She picked up her skirts and mounted the steps.

"And I am astonished to find you here," he returned coolly. "I thought you well on your way to Scotland by now."

"Scotland? How did you—?"

"I called early at the hotel only to be informed that you and your maid had taken off in the middle of the night. The porter had heard Scotland mentioned."

"I did think of going to Scotland," she confessed, "but I came here to collect my things and we overturned in the beck. Did you see Alfred?"

"I assumed he had gone to Scotland with you or at least was bound in the same direction."

"Why would he do that?" she asked in bewilderment.

"When two people elope they generally contrive to travel in the same direction."

"You thought we were bound for Gretna." Lilac stared at him. "I explained about Alfred."

"You had also agreed to marry me," he said dryly. "I had no reason to believe you told the truth about anything."

"I did mean to marry you," she protested. "Then I realised I loved you so much that I couldn't possibly let you take the risk. I decided to go to Scotland because I was sure you would not think of looking for me there. Later I'd have returned to London."

"It never entered your head that I wouldn't look for you at all?"

They were still standing in the hall. Her mouth formed a circle of dismay as she stared at him.

"You didn't even check at Sladen Hall as to whether I might have gone back there?" she said in a small voice.

"When a young lady flees from my vicinity in the middle of the night leaving clear word that she is bound for the north, I don't chase her like a lovesick schoolboy," he said curtly.

"I couldn't let you take the risk of my turning out like Robert Morton," Lilac gulped. "If I had loved you less it wouldn't have troubled me so much."

"Am I to take your arrival here now signifies that you love me less?" he asked.

"I found this, or rather Elijah found it, buried in the lilac garden." She thrust the paper at him. "It was in a tin box in my mother's hand. Read it. You will see that there is no risk at all, for I am Mark Sladen's daughter."

"Mark's daughter!"

He seized the letter and walked into the large room where she had stood that first night, dripping on the carpet.

"Sit down and hold your tongue until I have found out the truth of this," he ordered.

Lilac obeyed meekly, her eyes on his face as he read and reread the missive. At last he looked at her. "Mark was a year older than myself," he said. "That year we saw less of each other than usual. My grandfather had just died. I was almost eighteen and intent on proving I was a man. Mark was busy about his own affairs. I met your mother as I told you, but it was very briefly. I had no idea that she and Mark . . . Then I went away to stay with friends, a shooting party, and by the time I returned the tragedy was over. Robert Morton was hanged, and Mary had gone back to her mother. Mrs Lameter wrote to the vicar the following year to tell him that Mary and the child had died. Mark said nothing even then."

"He never found the letter."

"Poor Lilac." He looked across at her. "If only this had been known before, you would not have lost your lieutenant."

"Had I known about the murder before," she said, "I think I would have permitted him to take the risk of wedding me. I wanted to be loved, you see, but I hadn't yet learned how—not in a grown-up way."

"And now you do?"

"If you don't mind taking a girl who is not precisely . . . legitimate?"

"I will take you, Lilac Mary Morton, in any condition," he said and, dropping the letter, pulled her into his arms.

"Alfred will be looking for me," she remembered after a few moments of bliss. "He will be riding off to Scotland in the belief—"

"I guessed that was a blind designed to lead me astray."

Alfred's voice in the doorway made them both jump. He was somewhat dishevelled, his boots splashed with mud. "I slept late, but when I woke and discovered you had left the previous night I guessed that Harland would force you back here. I never should have allowed him to escort you home. As it is, I shall have the greatest pleasure in calling you out, sir. My seconds will call upon you to choose a time and place at your convenience."

"Oh, Alfred," Lilac was torn between mirth and consternation. "Don't be so foolish! Chance has not forced me anywhere. Haven't you been to Sladen Hall?"

"I rode here like the wind," Alfred said. "He hasn't abducted you?"

"He wasn't even looking for me," Lilac said. "We are going to be wed, Alfred, so you don't have to issue any challenges."

"Oh." Alfred sat down abruptly and turned crimson.

"Actually you are under a slight misapprehension," Chance said. "I have already sent two constables hotfoot to Gretna with orders to put a stop to any marriage a certain Miss Morton may try to contract on the grounds that she is still a minor and needs permission from her guardian. I was told it might prove difficult to effect such action. However, I was determined that before you wed anybody, you would hear from me that I was determined to marry you no matter who you are or who your parents may have been. You are twined round my heart in a damnably uncomfortable manner, and I intend to have you. That is loving, Miss Morton."

His bronze eyes were golden with mischievous laughter, matching the smile in her own as she said, "Aye, Mr Chance, that it is."

If you have enjoyed this book and would like to receive details of other Walker Regency romances, please write to:

Regency Editor
Walker and Company
720 Fifth Avenue
New York, N.Y. 10019